His wife…. Yes, that was what she was. But in name only….

Could she actually change this situation by having Nick make love to her? Gemini knew she would do anything to try to salvage their marriage. Anything at all…. He was so good-looking, Gemini groaned inwardly. The darkness of his hair was ruffled, the hard planes of his face softened by the muted lighting in the room, the warmth of his body seeming to reach out and enfold her.

"Gemini…?" he questioned uncertainly, his gaze narrowed on her flushed face. Flushed because she wanted Nick, wanted him so much she physically ached with it. And the way things stood between them, she knew she had little to lose! Besides, she was Nick's wife, damn it, and if any woman was entitled to share his bed, it was her! She would not give Nick up without a fight!

CAROLE MORTIMER says, "I was born in England, the youngest of three children—I have two older brothers. I started writing in 1978, and have now written over one hundred books for Harlequin Presents®.

"I have four sons, Matthew, Joshua, Timothy and Peter, and a bearded collie called Merlyn. I'm very happily married to Peter senior. We're best friends as well as lovers, which is probably the best recipe for a successful relationship. We live on the Isle of Man."

Books by Carole Mortimer

HARLEQUIN PRESENTS®
2086—A MAN TO MARRY
2098—THEIR ENGAGEMENT IS ANNOUNCED
2130—BOUND BY CONTRACT
2141—A YULETIDE SEDUCTION

Carole Mortimer

TO MEND A MARRIAGE

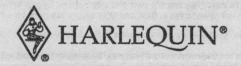

TORONTO • NEW YORK • LONDON
AMSTERDAM • PARIS • SYDNEY • HAMBURG
STOCKHOLM • ATHENS • TOKYO • MILAN • MADRID
PRAGUE • WARSAW • BUDAPEST • AUCKLAND

My husband,
Peter

ISBN 0-373-12152-0

TO MEND A MARRIAGE

First North American Publication 2001.

Copyright © 2000 by Carole Mortimer.

CHAPTER ONE

A BABY!

On her doorstep!

This couldn't be happening. There must be some sort of mistake. And it certainly hadn't been made by her!

Gemini continued to look blankly at the woman standing beside the carrycot, cursing the fact it was the housekeeper's day off. She had no doubts that Mrs James would have dealt with this situation in her usual capable manner—probably without bothering Gemini with it at all!

As it was, Gemini had been caught completely off guard when she'd opened the door herself, answering the ring of the doorbell, and found this other woman standing on her doorstep. With a baby in a carrycot she claimed she was here to deliver to Gemini!

Gemini shook her head confidently, dark shoulder-length hair swinging silkily against her cheeks. 'I never did believe that story about the stork,' she said dryly. 'And I hate to disappoint you, but I think there's been some sort of mistake—'

'No mistake,' the other woman assured her happily. 'Jemima gave me detailed instructions of how to get here, and exactly who I was to leave the baby with. After seeing you, I would have been in no doubt anyway.' The young woman laughed. 'The two of you are identical!'

Gemini had stopped listening the moment her twin sister's name was mentioned, although she stiffened resentfully as the last remark registered. She and Jemima might be identical in looks, but there the similarity ended!

But if her twin *were* behind this woman's presence here, Gemini knew she'd better listen to what she had to say...!

She stepped back, holding the door open. 'Perhaps you had better come inside,' she sighed. 'And bring—the baby with you,' she added reluctantly, not sure if the baby were a boy or a girl—and not particularly interested either way!

'I'm Janey Reynolds, by the way. Jessica's nanny,' the other woman said chattily as they walked down the thickly carpeted hallway. Janey carried the bulky carrycot in front of her, releasing its weight onto the sofa once they were in Gemini's sitting-room, and then looked about the obviously wealthy comfort of the room with interest.

'Gemini Stone,' she introduced herself vaguely, staring at the carrycot as if it were an alien being. Which it was, to her. She had no children of her own. And she wasn't particularly interested in any her sister might have produced, either!

Or perhaps this was all just someone's idea of a joke. But it was June, not April, and she didn't think any of her friends were crazy enough to involve a baby in any prank they pulled on her. Although she only had Janey Reynolds' word for it that there was a baby in the carrycot; maybe it was empty, and just another part of the joke...?

'Beautiful, isn't she?' Janey Reynolds prompted as Gemini leant cautiously over the side of the carrycot.

She looked like any other baby as far as Gemini was concerned: very pink, very wrinkled, with sparse dark hair—and, thankfully, at this moment her eyes were closed in sleep!

Gemini moved away from the cot as if she had been stung. There was definitely a baby in there. And if this woman were to be believed her sister was involved in its existence.

'Am I to take it you work for my sister, Jemima?' She looked at the younger woman with narrowed eyes.

Janey Reynolds looked to be in her early twenties, with an open, friendly face, lightly sprinkled with freckles, and reddish-blonde hair that was brushed back from that gamine face. Her slender figure was clothed in a tee shirt and fitted denims. Ideal wear for looking after a baby.

Whereas Gemini's own clothes—a silk blouse the same cobalt blue as her eyes and black silk trousers contoured to the tall slenderness of her body had been designed by Gemini herself, to be fashionable as well as comfortable. But, being silk, they were certainly not baby-proof. 'As Jessica's nanny,' Janey nodded, still smiling. 'I would've thought Jemima would have mentioned that to you...?' She frowned slightly.

As Gemini and Jemima hadn't seen each other for well over a year now, and the baby in the carrycot looked very young indeed, there wasn't much likelihood of that. In fact, if her sums were correct, Jemima couldn't even have been pregnant the last time they'd met. Which begged the question—who was the baby's father...?

'Please, sit down,' Gemini invited coolly, sitting down in the armchair opposite the other woman. 'Have you worked for my sister for very long?' she queried lightly, feeling totally in the dark here; she hadn't even known there was a baby, let alone how old it was!

Janey shook her head. 'Since the day she came out of the nursing-home. About six weeks,' she supplied as Gemini still looked blank.

'I see,' she said slowly—not seeing anything at all.

Jemima had given birth six weeks ago.... It seemed incredible that her twin could have gone through pregnancy, and then childbirth, without Gemini knowing anything about it. Of course, the emotional connection they'd used to have as children had gone long ago, but even so Gemini thought she would have felt something!

Janey looked a little less sure of herself now. 'Jemima

has been delayed in the States for the weekend at least,' she said slowly. 'I would have thought she'd have called you?'

'Called me?' Gemini was totally at a loss now.

Not only had she not seen Jemima for over a year, the two of them hadn't spoken to each other on the telephone, either; the rift between them was just too deep. Why on earth should Janey Reynolds assume that they might have spoken to each other now. Although the obvious answer to that was that the younger woman wasn't aware there *was* a rift. Typical of Jemima!

'About looking after Jessica for a few days until she returns,' Janey explained with a frown. 'You see—'

'What!' Gemini got up abruptly, totally aghast as what the other woman had just said. She stood as tall as any model, with the sort of slender figure that showed clothes well. Except she didn't model clothes; she designed them. GemStone was becoming one of the leading designer labels in the world, and Gemini herself was one of the best show-pieces for her own clothes: tall, elegant, with a cool beauty the press found as photogenic as each of her new collections.

But that cool beauty was definitely ruffled at the moment—when was it ever anything else when her sister was involved?

'I'm sure you must have misunderstood Jemima,' she told the other woman, pleasantly enough, determined not to become panicked. If she could manage to design and organise a new collection of clothes every season, she could definitely handle this—whatever this might be!

'I don't think so.' Janey shook her head, still frowning. 'As I said, Jemima has been delayed in America—'

'I understood that bit,' Gemini assured her coolly. 'I simply don't see what that delay has to do with me. You informed me that you are Jessica's nanny—'

'Oh, I am.' Janey Reynolds had started to look upset now. 'But it's my wedding day tomorrow.' She gave a self-conscious smile, 'So I obviously can't take care of Jessica until Jemima does return. Your sister assured me that it would be no problem for you to look after Jessica for a few days.' She chewed worriedly on her bottom lip at this last disclosure.

Of course it would be no problem for Jemima if her baby were left with Gemini—it was Gemini who had the problem with it. For one thing, she knew absolutely nothing about taking care of babies, and secondly, this latest escapade was just typical of Jemima—too busy with her own life to take care of her own responsibilities!

'Do you have a telephone number in America where Jemima might be reached?' she prompted impatiently. 'I'm sure if we speak to her this can all be sorted out in a matter of minutes.' Because Gemini would insist that her sister get herself back here, delay or no delay, and take care of her own daughter!

Janey looked pained. 'She's following through some story or other, and she's usually the one to call me...'

Gemini wondered just how often 'usually' was where her journalist sister was concerned; Jemima was dogged when it came to her work, and stopped at nothing to acquire an exclusive. Or anything else she wanted, for that matter. As Gemini knew to her cost...!

'Just how long has my sister been in America?' she questioned shrewdly.

'Almost a week,' Janey revealed reluctantly.

Unbelievable, when her baby was obviously so young. Although anything was possible with Jemima. 'So you have no way of contacting her.' Gemini spoke almost to herself. 'And it's your wedding day tomorrow, so naturally you aren't going to be around to take care of the baby for some time...' She looked questioningly at the nanny.

'I'm going on a two-week honeymoon to Barbados,' Janey replied, obviously aware by now that her presence here, with Jemima's baby, was a complete surprise to Gemini.

Gemini should have known; only Jemima would take on for her baby a nanny who was going on holiday mere weeks after being employed!

But none of this mental berating of her sister changed the fact that there was a six-week-old baby that needed looking after—or the fact that Gemini, as her aunt, was the one expected to do it!

At twenty-nine, Gemini had never even considered having any children of her own. She was a career woman, through and through, her designs the only 'babies' she was interested in.

Although now it looked as if, for a few days at least, she might have to take an interest in a six-week-old baby called Jessica!

Jemima really did have the most colossal damn cheek; the rift between the two sisters had been abrupt and final, over a year ago. How on earth did Jemima have the nerve to dump her baby on Gemini now after the way she had behaved then...?

Of course, it didn't help that she knew Nick was going to be absolutely furious about the situation.

Oh, damn Nick, *and* what he thought of the situation. If he were around as much this weekend as he had been the last few months he wouldn't even know she'd ever had a baby in the house, let alone that it was Jemima's!

She wasn't seriously contemplating looked after Jessica herself, was she. She knew nothing about babies, not how to feed them or look after them, and at only six weeks old she was sure Jessica was going to need a lot of both. Besides, she was Jemima's baby...!

No, the idea was utterly ridiculous. She couldn't do it.

'I suppose it's too late to engage a temporary nanny for the baby until Jemima comes back...?' she asked, frowning.

Janey grimaced. 'At six o'clock on a Friday evening? Not much chance, I would have thought.' She shrugged.

Then why hadn't she brought the baby here earlier. Damn it—

Jemima.... Her sister was the one who'd instructed Janey on what she was to do, so no doubt the timing of it had been planned by Jemima too. She didn't doubt for a moment that her irresponsible sister, in spite of the rift between the two of them, would think of it all as a big joke, would find the image of Gemini trying to cope with her very young daughter absolutely hilarious.

'I'm really sorry about this, Miss Stone.' Janey Reynolds had obviously realised by now that, in spite of what Jemima might or might not have told her, there was something very wrong here.

Gemini shook her head. 'You can be assured that I am well aware that none of this—situation is of your doing.' She sighed. 'I think you'd better go and get the rest of Jessica's things in from the car.' And there was probably going to be a lot of them for a baby as young as Jessica. 'I'm sure you must be anxious to be on your way,' she added flatly, wondering how she was going to cope. But at the same time she knew that Jemima had left her little choice.

Considering Jemima's dedication to her own career, Gemini couldn't even begin to imagine what had made her sister go ahead and have this baby. Admittedly Jemima had always been the one who, when they were children, had stayed indoors and played with her dolls, while Gemini had been climbing trees with the neighbours' sons, but it seemed as though Jessica's birth was just a mere hiccup in Jemima's life, a small inconvenience before she resumed following her own pursuits.

Janey hesitated on her way out to the car. 'Jessica is due for a feed in a few minutes; would you like me to stay and show you how to make the formula up, and give her the bottle...?'

Considering this young woman must have many other things on her mind at this time, Gemini appreciated the offer. And took unashamed advantage of it. It wasn't going to help anyone if, in her complete ignorance concerning the care of babies, she did it all wrong and made the baby ill!

It looked simple enough as she watched Janey do it—even the nappy changing didn't seem that horrendous. And immediately after her feed and change Jessica went back to sleep. Nothing to it!

'Er—I'll leave you my telephone number, if you like?' Janey seemed reluctant to go once the time came—obviously realising Gemini was a complete novice when it came to babies, and probably fearing for Jessica's safety.

Which was more than could be said for Jemima, Gemini inwardly berated. She would take great pleasure in thinking of suitable retribution for her sister over the weekend; this had to be the worst thing Jemima had ever done to her!

Well...almost, she remembered hardily.

And as for taking care of the baby..! If Jemima thought she had landed Gemini with something she couldn't handle, then she was going to be in for a big disappointment.

'That's very kind of you.' She accepted Janey's offer, putting her card next to the telephone. 'But I'm sure I won't be needing it,' she added confidently.

Four hours later she wasn't so sure about that. It had all looked so easy when Janey had fed and changed the baby, but actually putting that theory into practice proved much more difficult to Gemini than it had looked!

For one thing Gemini couldn't seem to get the hang of holding the baby while trying to feed her at the same time. And then the nappy didn't seem to want to stay on. In the

end she secured it into place by the poppers on Jessica's
bodyvest.

But finally, over an hour later—much longer than it
had taken Janey Reynolds!—the baby had been fed
and changed and was back asleep in her carrycot, giving
Gemini the chance to catch up on some of her own chores
before going to bed herself.

But it seemed no sooner had she fallen asleep than she
was woken up again by Jessica's whimpering cry from the
spare bedroom. And those slight whimpers grew to enor-
mous proportions before Gemini could wake herself up
enough to deal with it.

How on earth did new mothers cope with this for weeks,
sometimes months at a time? Gemini wondered as she
stumbled about the kitchen, trying to hold Jessica wrapped
in a shawl in one arm and warm the bottle with the other
hand.

Not that holding the baby stopped her crying. The noise
Jessica was making now seemed to go straight through
Gemini's head, reverberating around the kitchen.

But at last the bottle was warmed and she sat down
thankfully on one of the chairs around the kitchen table to
give the baby her milk. Only to find Jessica didn't want it,
pushing the bottle repeatedly from her lips with her little
pink tongue, and beginning that nerve-shattering wail once
again!

Gemini's nerves were already fraught from the crying—
now what did she do. Her first instinct was to telephone
Janey Reynolds and find out the answer to that. But a
glance at the clock showed her it was one o'clock in the
morning, hardly a very sociable time to be telephoning anyone!

One o'clock...?

Janey had said the baby fed approximately every four

hours, and it was only three hours since Jessica's last feed, even less than that from when she had first begun to cry.

Was Jessica sick? Did she have a temperature? What—?

'What the hell is going on here?'

Gemini looked up with a start, staring towards the doorway, wincing as she saw her husband standing there. Just what she needed when she was so harassed, and definitely looking less than her best.

When had he arrived home? Some time ago, by the look of him; he was obviously naked beneath the black silk robe he had belted about his waist, his dark hair ruffled from sleep.

A robe was a luxury she hadn't allowed herself when she'd hurried out of bed earlier to see to Jessica; she was wearing only pale grey silk pyjamas, and the baby had spat most of her milk down them in her distress!

So much for thinking earlier that Nick would probably never know there had ever been a baby in the house!

Gemini stood up abruptly, stilling holding the baby, whose wails seemed to have turned to hiccuping sobs now. 'What does it look like?' she snapped, showing her impatience with the question.

Nick blinked, green eyes narrowing in his ruggedly handsome face. 'It looks like a baby—but I'm sure this must all be just a bad dream; we don't have a baby!'

Considering that she and Nick had been married for more than a year now, and had occupied separate bedrooms from the beginning of their marriage, that was highly unlikely.

She and Nick had what could only be termed a business marriage, a marriage that suited both of them. At least, it had a year ago. She wasn't so sure that was the case now. For either of them. But for different reasons...

'That's very astute of you, Nick,' she drawled mockingly. 'Although it doesn't help in solving the problem of how to stop Jessica crying!' she added raggedly as the baby continued to wail. 'I wasn't expecting you home yet,' she added accusingly.

'I completed my business early,' he dismissed distractedly, striding into the kitchen with his usual ease of movement, taking the baby from her unresisting hands, frowning down into the little heart-shaped face. 'What's the matter, Jessica?' he murmured soothingly to the baby. 'We can't help you if you—' He stopped, frowning across at the watching Gemini. 'Have you tried changing her nappy?'

Gemini watched in fascination as her tall, arrogant husband strolled about the kitchen carrying the slightness that was Jessica. He was one of the most handsome men Gemini had ever set eyes on, possessed of a physical magnetism that she'd been unaware of when they first married.

When had that changed?

She wasn't really sure. She only knew that she felt a deep sense of dissatisfaction in their marriage now, a longing for something more.

'Gemini!' Nick prompted, impatient with receiving no response to his question of a few minutes ago.

She bristled resentfully. 'Janey said not to change her nappy until after the feed—'

'And I'm sure that Janey—whoever she might be!—is probably correct about the usual order of things—if it weren't for the fact that Jessica is extremely damp!' Nick grimaced as he pointedly peeled back the shawl the baby was wrapped in to reveal her sleepsuit was soaking wet!

Gemini felt the hot colour enter her cheeks, feeling a total sense of inadequacy where this baby was concerned. And not being in control of a situation was something she wasn't in the least comfortable with. Especially around Nick!

She hadn't even thought to check the baby's nappy when she'd got Jessica up a short time ago and wrapped her in the shawl. Instead she'd been intent only on warming the bottle so that the baby would stop crying. Except that she hadn't..! And the reason for that was now obvious.

It was even more so once Gemini had stripped off the wet clothing to find that the nappy she had had such difficulty with at the last feed had somehow moved sideways while Jessica slept. The nappy itself was almost dry, leaving Jessica's clothes very wet. And the situation was made all the worse by the fact that all the time she was undressing the baby Nick was watching her actions with those mocking green eyes narrowed, making her feel more inadequate than ever.

She would never forgive Jemima for this!

'Here, let me,' Nick muttered impatiently, obviously tired of her efforts to replace the nappy and taking over the task himself, achieving an almost perfect result within seconds. Much to Gemini's chagrin. Was there nothing that Nick wasn't totally competent at?

'When did you get to be such an expert on babies?' she muttered resentfully as Nick put Jessica's clean clothes on seemingly without effort, too. The baby was clean and dry minutes later, the crying having stopped as she began to fall back to sleep cradled in Nick's strong, comforting arms.

'I'm no expert, Gemini,' Nick drawled derisively. 'I just used a little common sense. Besides...' He shrugged. 'I'm ten years older than Danny; I used to enjoy helping out with him when I was a child.'

Gemini stiffened at the mention of his younger brother. By tacit agreement neither she nor Nick had talked about Danny or Jemima since the first day of their own marriage. The reason for that was simple enough; there had been nothing left to say about either of them.

And Gemini couldn't help but be surprised at Nick mentioning Danny now...

Although it did give her the perfect opening for her next comment...! 'Nick, Jessica is Jemima's baby,' she told him baldly, her gaze narrowing as she watched closely for his reaction to the announcement.

There wasn't one. At least, not one that he allowed to be visible to Gemini. But that was typical of Nick, too. Her husband was a man who showed little emotion about anything except the mockery that seemed to be such a natural part of his nature. Although Gemini was sure that inside he had to be churning with some sort of emotion. He had to be!

Because if all their lives hadn't been turned upside down fifteen months ago by Jemima's selfishness, *he* could have been Jessica's father...!

CHAPTER TWO

'I SUGGEST we put the baby back to bed and you can tell me what the hell you're talking about!' Nick rasped now, his mouth tight.

Gemini could completely sympathise with his feelings. Fifteen months ago Nick had been her sister Jemima's fiancé, a little fact her sister seemed to have forgotten when she'd seen someone else that she wanted! And her engagement to Nick hadn't been the only thing Jemima had conveniently forgotten!

'Shouldn't I feed the baby first?' she prompted uncertainly; after all, it was now four hours since Jessica's last feed.

'Hardly!' Nick gave a pointed look at the sleeping baby.

Gemini could feel that heated colour enter her cheeks once again. Damn it, she was usually so cool and in control, especially around Nick, who was always so competent himself; it was totally unfair that she found herself in this unfamiliar role with him as a witness!

And she didn't feel any more comfortable with the situation as the two of them placed the baby back into her carrycot and arranged the blankets over her. They looked like a pair of doting parents, for goodness' sake—and, considering the sterile state of their marriage, that was something they would never be!

'Time for a brandy, I think,' Nick muttered grimly once they had settled the baby back in her cot in the spare bedroom.

'I'll just get my robe,' Gemini told him lightly, ever conscious of the fact that she was only wearing the milk-stained pyjamas.

Nick gave her a mocking sideways glance. 'I've seen women in less, Gemini,' he drawled derisively.

She flicked her hair back, her chin raised haughtily. 'Not me, you haven't,' she snapped.

'True,' he murmured mockingly. 'But it's a fact you are my wife...'

She knew what she was. Didn't need any reminding. Nor did she need to be reminded of the fact that there had been other women in Nick's life before he married her.

And since...?

She'd tried over recent months not to think too deeply about Nick's private life. Before that it hadn't occurred to her to think about it; it was only lately she had begun to wonder—

No! These were thoughts that took her nowhere—except to sleepless nights as she lay torturing herself with wondering whether or not Nick really *was* away on business, or if there could be some other reason, *someone*, who kept him away from home for days at a time!

It was an aspect of their marriage they hadn't discussed when they'd decided to marry each other fourteen months ago. It hadn't occurred to Gemini at the time to discuss it; if she'd thought about it she'd probably assumed that Nick would make his own arrangements. It was only in recent months that Gemini had found herself thinking about that side of his life too...

Because, as she knew only too well, Nick was a very attractive man, and it would be ridiculous to assume that he had remained celibate during their marriage. And it certainly hadn't been *her* he was making love to...!

Damn it, she didn't want to think about that, had no right to do so. They had married each other for their own reasons, and they weren't reasons that allowed for interference in each other's private lives.

Nick had poured the brandies when Gemini joined him in the sitting-room, its gas-flame fire adding a cheeriness to the room. Which was just as well, because Nick's grim expression wasn't in the least cheering!

'So, true to form, Jemima has done it again—only this time she's dumped her baby on you?' he rasped without preamble.

'Not exactly.' Gemini grimaced, taking her glass of brandy to sip it gratefully; she should have guessed Nick would get straight to the point! 'What I mean is that, yes, Jessica has been brought here, but it wasn't by Jemima. You see—'

'No—I don't see,' he cut in with icy disdain. 'But then, where your irresponsible sister is concerned—does anybody?'

Gemini wasn't even going to attempt to defend her twin sister. She simply couldn't imagine two people more unalike than Jemima and herself; Jemima roamed the world in search of the latest scoop, very rarely in the same place for any length of time, whereas Gemini had lived in London all of her life, dedicatedly etching out a career for herself in the world of fashion.

No, she couldn't say she understood her twin's need for travel and excitement, but by the same token she *was* her sister...

'Jemima is in America,' she told Nick evenly. 'The young lady she engaged as Jessica's nanny is going to be married tomorrow, and so obviously she can't look after her at the moment—'

'Obviously,' Nick acknowledged disgustedly.

Gemini drew in a deep, controlling breath, knowing his anger was well merited; Jemima was going to hear exactly what she thought of her when she returned. When...!

'But the nanny has assured me that Jemima should be back on Monday,' she added, more with hope than any degree of certainty; if Jemima didn't have her story by then, there was no telling when she would be back!

'And so she's left you here holding her baby—literally?' Nick dismissed scathingly.

She frowned. 'Admittedly, it's a little inconvenient—'

'Inconvenient!' Nick echoed, shaking his head disgustedly. 'Considering the two of you haven't even spoken for well over a year, I find the whole thing incredible. I won't say unbelievable—because nothing your sister does surprises me any more!' he added grimly.

He still cared, Gemini realised with dismay. It had been almost fifteen months since Jemima had broken her engagement to him so thoughtlessly, but it was obvious from the bitterness Nick was showing now that the insult had been far from forgotten. Or forgiven...

And why should it be—wasn't it for that very reason that she and Nick were now married to each other...?

Nick's romance with Jemima had happened so suddenly and so quickly, sixteen months ago, that it had only been at the dinner to celebrate their engagement that the two of them had been introduced to each other's families. Both sets of parents were dead, and so it was left to Gemini, as Jemima's sister, and Danny, Nick's younger brother, to represent what little family there was left.

Gemini had been sceptical about the suddenness of the romance, believing it to be just another of Jemima's rash—and usually disastrous!—impulses. But to her surprise Nick Drummond had turned out to be exactly the sort of man every mother would wish their daughter to meet and marry: obviously wealthy, very handsome, with an arrogance that protected all of those close to him. And, as Nick's future wife, Jemima had definitely come into that category.

The only problem Gemini had been able to see with the

match had been that if anything Nick was just too perfect, too arrogant, too much in control of himself and those around him. Jemima, on the other hand, had been ten years younger than her new fiancé, full of fun and life, eager for excitement and adventure.

But the four of them had enjoyed a pleasant dinner together. Danny Drummond was ten years younger than his brother, a professional naturalist photographer who worked freelance for several well-known magazines. He was completely different from his brother in looks, a little under six feet in height, with overlong blonde hair and laughing brown eyes.

What should have been apparent to all of them that night was that Danny was also full of fun and life, eager for excitement and adventure...

Gemini had been bowled over by him, fascinated by his stories of trekking through Africa in his search for wildlife pictures that would appeal to others as well as himself, and at the end of the evening she'd been only too happy to accept his invitation for the two of them to have dinner together the following evening.

There had followed a month in Gemini's life the like of which she had never known before. Danny was completely unconventional; their dates had been equally so. Danny had even whisked her off to a Scottish island for the weekend on one occasion—because he'd wanted to film the birdlife there.

Gemini had been enthralled, enraptured, her own life and career put on hold every time Danny made one of his unannounced appearances. But it had all come to an abrupt end the day she had visited Danny's apartment and found Jemima there with him...!

She looked across at Nick now, remembering all too clearly the humiliated anger they had both felt at learning that her sister and his brother had been indulging in a little relationship of their own behind their backs...

'I should have known, damn it,' Nick muttered to himself now.

Gemini gave him a puzzled look. 'Should have known what?'

He looked as if he were about to explode with anger. 'Jemima called me today—'

'Jemima did?' Gemini cut in angrily; the last she had heard of Jemima and Nick's friendship they hadn't even been talking to each other! And now it appeared Jemima was telephoning him...!

He nodded. 'On my mobile. Apparently she tried to call the house this morning—'

'I was out shopping,' Gemini said dazedly. Her sister had called Nick on his mobile...! For the first time in the last year. Or had Jemima contacted him before in this way?

Nick's mouth twisted. 'And Mrs James was away for the day,' he realised. 'Jemima wanted to know if we would be at home this weekend. I assured her that we would,' he said grimly. 'I had no idea the reason she wanted to know was because she intended dumping her baby here!'

Well, at least Jemima's telephone call to Nick proved that her sister wasn't quite as irresponsible as she had thought her to be; at least she had ascertained that someone would be at home before Jessica was brought here!

But what else did it mean...? Was Jemima in the habit of calling Nick on his mobile? Despite the fact he was her husband, Gemini simply didn't have the sort of relationship with Nick that would allow her to ask him such a question.

'If it's not too stupid a question—who the hell is the father?' Nick rasped, with a return of that cold, remorseless anger that had become such a part of him fifteen months ago on learning of Jemima and Danny's duplicity.

And the question wasn't so unreasonable, either—because two months after Jemima had broken her engagement to Nick, because she'd supposedly been in love with Danny, she and Danny had also parted!

But it had been too late then for any second thoughts on Gemini or Nick's part—because they had already been married to each other…

She wasn't naturally impulsive by nature—she believed Jemima must have inherited all that part of their character at their birth—but at the time there had been no doubt in Gemini's mind that she had fallen in love with Danny Drummond, hook, line and sinker. Only to find that he had been having an affair with Jemima almost from the very first evening they had all been introduced!

Gemini had been devastated by both Danny and Jemima's behaviour. Nick's reaction to his brother and fiancée's duplicity had been much less predictable—he'd asked Gemini to marry him!

Her initial reaction to the proposal had been one of disbelief. And a questioning as to why, after being hurt so badly, she should want to marry anyone!

But even as she had asked herself that question she had known the answer all too clearly; all of her friends and business acquaintances had known of her relationship with Danny, of how for one wild, impetuous month she had put the rest of her life on hold to be with him—even GemStone had taken second place to the relationship for a while. She was going to look a complete idiot, both privately and professionally, when it became public knowledge that Danny had actually preferred her sister!

But she'd been sure Nick couldn't be serious about the proposal, that it was just a knee-jerk reaction to Jemima's betrayal. But he was quite serious, Nick had assured her grimly. Why shouldn't they marry each other? They were both adults, and falling in love had proved a humiliating experience for both of them. And he was thirty-eight, he'd stated, it was time he had a wife, and Gemini, successful, self-assured, wise now to the stupidity of falling in love, would make him a very good one. And she, he'd claimed, would gain a husband who made no emotional demands on her, who was proud of her achievements and, most importantly of all, would never hurt or humiliate her in the way Danny had.

It had been this last claim, a brutal reminder of how ridiculous she was going to look to the outside world, and feeling still deeply wounded by the hurt Danny and Jemima had inflicted on her, that had made her make the last impulsive decision of her life and say yes!

Nick had kept to his word, and their marriage of fourteen months was undoubtedly a success in all that it had set out to be. Gemini was there as Nick's partner and hostess if he should need one, and Nick was there for her in the same guise. And the existence of their marriage had completely taken away any public sting of humiliation they might have encountered after the end of their relationships with Danny and Jemima. To all intents and purposes it had looked as if the two of *them* had been the ones to realise they had previously made a mistake, and those mistakes had been rectified by the two of them marrying each other.

Yes, their marriage had succeeded in everything it had set out to do. Gemini had long ago recovered from the hurt Danny had so selfishly inflicted on her heart, having realised it had been a brief infatuation. It was hardly Nick's fault if she was now fully aware—inwardly, at least!—of her magnetic attraction to the man who was now her husband.

And now Jemima, selfish, uncaring Jemima, had calmly delivered her six-week-old baby into the marriage!

Gemini shook her head now in answer to Nick's question concerning Jessica's father. 'I have no idea,' she sighed. 'But the nanny who delivered the baby here earlier this evening didn't mention any man being involved,' she added with a frown.

'Not for some months, at least,' Nick bit out contemptuously. 'I can't believe I was ever stupid enough to believe I actually loved the woman!' he added self-disgustedly before throwing the brandy to the back of his throat, seemingly unmoved as the fiery liquid hit his stomach.

Gemini winced. Not because she didn't feel the same anger towards Jemima for this last thoughtlessness, but because she could no longer bear the thought of Nick ever having been in love with Jemima...

Quite how these possessive feelings towards her own husband had occurred Gemini wasn't aware, but she had found in recent months that what had begun as a purely business arrangement was no longer so. At least on her part.

But Nick's angry response to Jemima's latest escapade seemed to imply he was still in love with her sister.

'How can the two of you be identical to look at and yet be so unalike in temperament?' he added with a disbelieving shake of his head.

Jemima was beautiful, warm and funny, if irresponsible. Gemini, as the eldest twin, if only by minutes, was more serious, coolly detached and self-assured, and dedicated to promoting her own fashion label.

And it was obvious which of them Nick found the most attractive!

God, how that hurt. How could she have been stupid enough to fall in love with her own husband?

Because that was exactly what she'd done. She wasn't even sure when or how; she only knew that she had, that every time he was at home she was totally aware of him, that she found the way he looked physically attractive, that she admired the successful way he ran his business empire. In fact, she loved everything about him! And at the same time she knew that he felt no more for her now than he had when he had first proposed this sterile marriage fourteen months ago...

Gemini stood up abruptly. 'I don't think getting into a character assassination—' or otherwise! '—is going to help the situation,' she told Nick briskly, smoothing down the silkiness of her grey silk robe, very aware of the fact that she had cleansed her face before going to bed and so consequently wore no make-up, that her hair was probably in disarray too.

In fact, she probably looked a fright! And the one thing she had been very decided on, when accepting Nick's proposal of marriage, was that she would always make sure to keep her end of their bargain, that she would never be less than the beautiful showpiece and perfect hostess that he wanted in his marriage.

Nick's mouth twisted. 'You're probably right—talking about the flaws in Jemima's character could take all night!'

And Gemini had no wish to talk about her sister for the rest of the night. In fact, she had no real wish to talk about her sister at all. It was bad enough that she knew Nick still felt so strongly towards Jemima, without the two of them talking about her too!

'In that case,' she said coolly, 'I suggest the two of us get back to bed—' She broke off as Nick looked across at her with dark brows raised speculatively. 'Separately, of course,' she bit out tersely.

'Of course,' he drawled derisively.

Gemini glared at him. 'I'm tired, and not a little irritable; this certainly isn't the time for your warped sense of humour, Nick,' she snapped resentfully—because a part of her so wished he weren't joking at all.

She'd been aware the whole time they were talking that Nick was naked under that black silk robe, and just the thought made her ache!

It wasn't difficult to see that his shoulders were wide,

his body leanly muscled, and she could see the dark hair that grew on his chest, and the bareness of his legs beneath the robe. Just looking at him made Gemini's knees tremble with a need she had never known before! With anyone...

Strange, she had believed herself to be so much in love with Danny fifteen months ago. But after being Nick's wife for over a year she couldn't even remember what Danny looked like, let alone what it had felt like to be with him...

Nick's was such a strong personality, and he had so much physical presence, that when he wasn't at home the house seemed strangely empty, only coming alive again when he returned. As it had tonight...

'Sorry.' He grimaced now at her rebuke, running a hand through the dark thickness of his hair. 'I— What is it?' he prompted sharply at her indrawn breath.

How on earth could she possibly tell the man who was her husband that she longed to run *her* hands through the darkness of his hair, that she wanted to lie in bed next to him looking down at him, to kiss every part of him, to know the full pleasure she was sure Nick was capable of giving her; that she wanted to give him pleasure in return!

There was no way she could ever let him even see she felt that way, let alone tell him such a thing!

'Nothing,' she snapped abruptly. 'I told you, I'm tired.' She relented slightly as he raised dark brows at her unaccustomed aggression. He could hardly be blamed—or even know!—that the frustrated irritation she always felt nowadays when he was at home had returned. 'Did you have a good business trip?' she prompted as she moved to switch off some of the lamps prior to going to bed.

He shrugged. 'It was the usual round of business meetings,' he dismissed in a bored voice.

'It can't have been all business, Nick.' She attempted to tease him, still deeply troubled by the way Jemima had telephoned him—and whether or not it was something that had happened before!

He looked across at her with intense green eyes, not answering her for several minutes.

And Gemini couldn't help wondering if she had given herself away. Had her tone not been as teasing as she had meant it to be? Worse, had she sounded like a suspicious wife?

She hoped not; it was something she knew Nick would never tolerate. He never questioned her when she came back from buying trips, never showed the slightest interest in what she did on a social level while she was away from home.

Damn him!

Okay, so she wasn't Jemima, but the two of them were identical to look at, and before she'd known the Drummond brothers there had never been any shortage of men wanting to take her out, to tell her she was beautiful, desirable. Nor since, if she were honest...

So why didn't Nick find her attractive?

She'd asked herself that question so many times during recent months, and the only answer she had been able to come up with was that it was because she and Jemima *were* identical, and in Nick's eyes maybe she was only a pale copy of her twin sister.

Now that hurt!

Because she was a person in her own right. When they were children their mother had always dressed the two girls the same, styled their dark hair the same way, so much so that they had simply become known as 'the Stone twins'. But adulthood had brought deliberate changes, and the two women's styles of dress were now completely different. Jemima favoured jeans and tee shirts, while Gemini's clothes were always stylish and elegant. Jemima kept her

hair cropped short for convenience's sake; Gemini preferred a softer, shoulder-length style.

But Gemini knew she had to accept the fact that in
Nick's eyes it was the differences in their personalities that
left her wanting...

'No, not all business, Gemini,' he finally answered her
slowly, still watching her with narrowed eyes. '"All work
and no play", and all that rubbish...' he added derisively.

She swallowed hard, not knowing if she wanted to go
on with this conversation but also knowing it was too late
to stop now! 'And in what way do you "play" while you're
away, Nick?' She hoped she had managed to make her tone
sound light and uninterested this time! Sound it—because
it was far from the way she felt; her hands were clenched
so tightly at her sides that her nails were sticking into the
palms of her hands.

He bent to switch off the gas fire before answering her.
To give him time to think of a suitable answer? One that
would be acceptable to a wife? His wife?

But then she was his wife in name only, and not even
that really. Her fashion label GemStone meant that most
people still assumed her name was Gemini Stone, and not
Drummond at all...

'I spent a lot of time in the hotel pool,' he finally
drawled, his green gaze meeting hers challengingly.

Because he couldn't have spent every evening in the
swimming pool, and they both knew it! But to pursue this
subject any further would surely be dangerous on her part;
Nick would want to know the reason for her interest, and
there was no way she could tell him it was jealousy of the
time he spent with anyone else but her! Especially if that
'anyone' should turn out to be Jemima!

'That must have been nice.' She nodded, turning to
leave.

'Er—Gemini...?' Nick stopped her as she reached the door.

She froze, turning slowly back to face him. Had she given herself away, after all? She could read nothing from his closed expression. 'Yes?' she prompted warily.

'I hope you don't mind, but I've accepted a dinner invitation for the two of us with the Crawfords tomorrow evening,' he drawled pointedly.

The point was completely lost on her! Why should he think that would be a problem for her? She was always more than happy to go out with Nick. In fact, she looked forward to the evenings they would be out together in public; Nick was always the attentive husband on such occasions, and even though she knew it was a façade she still revelled in his protective care!

'Jessica...?' Nick reminded her as she continued to look blank. 'I don't think it would be quite the thing to take her along with us—do you?' he added mockingly.

The baby! She'd done it again, Gemini realised; of course, they would need a babysitter for Jessica if the two of them were to go out together!

'Perhaps Mrs James...?' She grimaced hopefully.

'We can ask her.' Nick nodded. 'Although I don't think that was part of her job description when I employed her ten years ago!'

Gemini was sure it wasn't. Rachel James was a woman in her late fifties, and while she used the title of Mrs she had confided in Gemini shortly after she'd come to live here as Nick's wife, that it was a courtesy title only, useful in the profession she had chosen for herself, but that she'd never actually been married.

Which meant she'd probably never had to deal much with children, either, and in particularly not a very young baby!

'I'll have a talk to her in the morning,' Gemini assured Nick dismissively. 'But I don't think Mrs James will mind.'

'No,' he acknowledged dryly. 'I had visions of there being problems with Mrs James when you came to live here as my wife,' he explained at Gemini's questioning look, 'but in fact it's turned out to be the opposite! Mrs James always comes to you for instructions,' he murmured ruefully. 'Fills the house with daffodils at all times of the year because she knows they're your favourite flower, prepares the meals she knows you like—'

'If any of that is a problem for you, Nick, you should have said,' Gemini put in uncomfortably; she hadn't even realised he had noticed those slight but subtle changes in the household.

She'd only mentioned once in passing to the housekeeper that she loved daffodils, that their golden colour always made her feel in a cheerful mood—and before she knew it the house was ablaze with the beautiful blooms. Just as she had once mentioned that she preferred to eat fish and chicken to red meat—only to find that red meat all but disappeared from their dining table!

'Oh, it isn't a problem, Gemini,' Nick assured her derisively. 'I merely look on in admiration at the charm you've exerted over our formerly austere housekeeper.'

It wasn't a question of charming the older woman; she merely treated Rachel James like a person. She hadn't grown up in a household that had had employees in the house of any kind. She'd lived on her own in a flat before marrying Nick. She wasn't accustomed to having staff in her home. Rachel had somehow sensed that in her, and had helped her all she could, forging a bond of understanding between the two women that Nick probably couldn't understand.

Nick raised dark brows. 'How is it you've never attempted to exert that charm over me...?' he prompted huskily.

Gemini gave him a sharp look. Was he flirting with her?

For the most part, Gemini and her husband lived together quite comfortably, with a friendly politeness between them. And Nick rarely, if ever, made any sort of remark that stepped over that line of friendship, that could be taken as being in the least flirtatious. And yet this evening he'd done so more than once...

Don't overreact, Gemini, she inwardly warned herself, her pulse beating fast, totally aware of every muscle and sinew of Nick's near-naked body, able to smell the aftershave that was such a part of him as he stood only feet away from her.

But it was very late, that time of the night when nothing seemed quite as it usually was, and Nick probably didn't mean anything at all by the remark he had just made. In fact, it was probably all the talk of Jemima that had prompted it!

She gave a self-deprecating smile. 'Probably because I know I would be wasting my time!'

'I wouldn't be too sure of that,' he murmured throatily.

'I would,' she assured him flatly, all too aware of how he felt about her sister.

'Why don't you try it and see?' he encouraged softly, seeming suddenly closer now, although Gemini hadn't been aware of him moving.

Gemini was more sure than ever that he was confusing her with Jemima. 'You don't really—' She broke off as she heard the sound of Jessica's whimpering cry coming from upstairs.

'Saved by the bell—or in this case the baby,' Nick drawled. 'I think Jessica has decided it's time for a feed, after all,' he muttered dryly.

And Gemini, for one, didn't know if she was relieved or disappointed at the interruption!

There was something different about Nick tonight, on his return from this business trip. He was exerting a sensuality over her that she would have to be totally uninterested not to be aware of—and she was far from being that!

'You warm a bottle and take it up to her; I'll turn the lights off down here when I come up,' Nick told Gemini briskly as he turned away, and that air of intimacy that had briefly been between them was totally dispelled at the return of his usual terseness.

Gemini grabbed the bottle from the kitchen and hurried up the stairs, all the time aware that Nick was still in the sitting-room, where she'd left him.

What had happened between them just now? she wondered as she fed the baby. And had it really happened *between* them, or had Nick briefly allowed her similarity to Jemima in looks to deceive him...?

Somehow—sadly—she had the feeling the latter was the true explanation...!

CHAPTER THREE

GEMINI couldn't believe it; her bedside clock read ten o'clock in the morning!

But it couldn't be. She'd last fed Jessica at two o'clock, and although she knew very little about babies, surely Jessica was too young yet to have gone through the eight hours from her last feed?

Oh, no. Was there something wrong with the baby?

Gemini's expression was frantic as she jumped out of bed and rushed to the spare bedroom—only to find the carrycot was empty!

But where was Jessica?

She felt sick as she rushed down the stairs. If anything had happened to the baby she would never forgive herself—

'Where's the fire?'

She turned sharply at the sound of Nick's mocking voice coming from the doorway of the breakfast-room, coming to an abrupt halt as she saw the sleeping baby in his arms, her tension leaving her so suddenly she felt like a deflated balloon.

She groaned, putting a shaky hand to her forehead. 'I thought Jessica had gone,' she admitted breathlessly, that sick feeling still in the pit of her stomach.

'She's a little young to have just walked out of here, don't you think?' Nick mocked.

'Very funny!' She raised her head to glare at him with angry blue eyes. 'I had no idea where she could have gone!'

'And now you can see that she's perfectly safe down

here with me,' he taunted, turning back into the breakfast-room, looking comfortable and relaxed in faded denims and a black shirt this morning. 'Come in here and have a cup of coffee; you know you aren't even halfway human until you've had your first cup of coffee of the morning!'

Living in such close proximity with this man meant he knew altogether too much about her, Gemini decided grumpily as she followed him into the breakfast-room and poured herself a cup of coffee. Because he was right, of course—when wasn't he?

Her first gulps of the rich brew were bringing back some feeling of equilibrium. She frowned as she looked up to find him watching her with an amused smile on his arrogant face as he sat opposite her at the table. 'It isn't funny, Nick,' she complained irritably.

'I wasn't laughing at you, Gemini—I was just thinking how sexy you look in pyjamas! And you blush delightfully, too!' he added teasingly as her cheeks coloured fiery red at the intimacy of the compliment.

Because it was no longer two o'clock in the morning—and Nick was still making flirtatious remarks!

She'd changed out of the grey milk-stained pyjamas when she'd finally got to bed last night, and was wearing another silk pair now, the same cobalt-blue as her eyes this time. And once again she hadn't had time to put a robe on over their silkiness!

Oh, damn it, after a year of being what she hoped was the perfect wife, always perfectly groomed and dressed, in the last twenty-four hours Nick had seen her not once, but twice, wearing only the pyjamas she favoured for sleeping in. It wasn't fair!

She pushed some of her hair impatiently back behind her ears as the silky softness fell about her face. 'I can't believe I slept until this time of the morning!' She couldn't remember the last time she had slept in later than eight o'clock.

Nick shrugged. 'Jessica woke at seven for a feed, and when I looked in on you you were sleeping so peacefully I just left you to it and fed her myself. It wasn't a problem.'

Nothing ever was with Nick; he always seemed able to cope with any situation that was thrown at him—including crying babies that needed feeding.

Strange, because when Gemini had first met him, albeit as Jemima's fiancé, her one worry about the relationship had been how Nick would cope if the two of them had children. He'd already been thirty-eight, his lifestyle firmly in place, and the arrival of children would definitely throw that routine out of the window! It hadn't been something she'd particularly thought about when the two of them had married instead—children weren't even a possibility when they occupied separate bedrooms!

But if the situation warranted it, as Jessica's needing a feed had this morning, Nick obviously felt no qualms about entering her bedroom...

She looked at the sleeping baby nestled in his arms, her expression softening as she saw the total vulnerability of such a tiny creature. She admired the way Nick held Jessica, so capably that the baby couldn't help but feel secure and loved.

Would she feel the same way if Nick held *her* like that...?

Gemini looked away abruptly, swallowing hard. 'You certainly do seem to have a way with babies—' She looked up questioningly at Nick as he began to chuckle softly.

'I thought you were going to say with females.' He dryly explained the reason for his humour.

'And just how would I know that?' Gemini came back waspishly, stung by the reference to other women.

Nick tilted his head questioningly to one side as he looked across at her, the intensity of that gaze making Gemini feel suddenly uncomfortable.

She'd said too much again! She seemed to have been doing rather a lot of that the last twenty-four hours, too. But the arrival of Jessica into their well-ordered existence seemed to have broken down those barriers of politeness that had separated them. Besides, it was very difficult to maintain a polite front when dressed only in revealing silk pyjamas—especially when Nick had already remarked that she looked sexy in them!

She stood up, pushing her chair back noisily. 'I think I'll go back upstairs and get dressed—'

'Gemini.' Nick softly cut across her rushed words of departure. 'If you ever want to change the terms of our marriage, you only have to say the words...'

She stood stricken to the spot, staring down at him. What words? He didn't seriously expect her to just blurt out that when she wasn't feverishly working, to keep her mind and body busy, she thought of little else but being in Nick's arms, of the two of them making love together?

If he did, then she really had said too much! And the last thing she wanted from Nick was his sympathy—or, even worse, that he should decide second best, in Jemima's twin, was better than nothing!

Gemini deliberately adopted a derisive expression. 'Really, Nick, if I ever feel the need of a man in that way there are dozens of available ones out there who would do just as well—and who'd cause far less complication!' she told him tauntingly.

His mouth tightened grimly, his eyes taking on a cold brilliance as he looked at her through a frown. 'I wouldn't recommend you try it, Gemini,' he warned softly.

She stiffened resentfully at his tone, drawing herself up to her full height of five feet eight inches in her bare feet.

'Would that be because you've already tried it yourself?' she challenged caustically.

'I—' His lips clamped together angrily as the housekeeper bustled into the room with a fresh pot of coffee. Nick continued to hold Gemini's gaze for several seconds more before allowing her to turn and look at Mrs James.

But those few seconds had been long enough for Gemini to know there had been more than advice in Nick's words; he had meant them as a warning.

But why? Their marriage was a polite façade at best, and at worst it had been a mistake, for both of them. At the time she'd accepted Nick's proposal she hadn't really thought further than saving their faces; over a year later she could see that they couldn't live the rest of their lives together in this same way...

'I thought I heard you, Mrs Drummond!' Rachel James greeted her warmly, putting down the pot of fresh coffee. 'What can I get you for breakfast this morning?'

The thought of any food, let alone the hearty breakfast their Scottish housekeeper thought Gemini ought to eat every morning in order to 'keep up her strength', made her feel ill after this most recent disturbing conversation with Nick!

'I'll probably have some toast later,' she said, smiling to dissipate the other woman's disappointment in her reply. 'I really do have to go upstairs and get dressed. You—' The baby, probably sensing that Nick was no longer as relaxed as he had been, began to stir in his arms, giving a little whimper of protest at having her sleep disturbed.

'Away with you and get yourself dressed,' Mrs James dismissed, taking the baby from Nick's arms. 'I'll take care of this little darling until you come down. We may as well get used to each other if I'm to look after her this evening while the two of you are out,' she assured them lightly, beginning to talk softly to Jessica as she left the room with her in her arms.

Gemini glanced awkwardly at Nick, knowing by his grim expression that he was still thinking about their last conversation. Well, so was she, and she hadn't liked the tone of his voice at all. She never questioned his private life—much as she might like to!—and she found his warning about hers more than a little arrogant. 'I see you've already spoken to Mrs James about this evening?' she said coolly, wondering how, with the tension that seemed to have sprung up between them, they were going to spend the evening in each other's company at all!

He nodded tersely. 'Apparently she loves children,' he bit out. 'She says she can't wait for us to have some of our own!' he added scornfully.

As the housekeeper, Rachel James must be well aware of the fact that they occupied separate bedrooms. Unless the older woman presumed that was only after they had made love…!

Gemini could imagine nothing worse than having her husband visit her in her bed and then return to his own room to go to sleep! She would rather leave the arrangement exactly as it was!

Her mouth twisted mockingly. 'Perhaps someone should tell her that isn't even a remote possibility!' she taunted.

Nick stood up abruptly, that very suddenness of movement meaning that his height and breadth seemed to dominate the room. 'You'll tell her no such thing!' he rasped furiously, his expression so ferocious Gemini took a step backwards, coming up against the partly open door.

She swallowed hard. 'I wasn't necessarily referring to me,' she told him irritably.

'Well, I certainly don't go around telling people my wife doesn't share my bed—or vice versa!' His green eyes blazed with fury.

Because not too many people would believe it, Gemini was sure. They were both fit and healthy, and obviously found the opposite sex attractive. Nick was a very handsome man, and she'd been told that she was beautiful; who would ever believe they'd lived together as husband and wife for over a year and never made love with each other?

She gave a weary sigh. 'We seem to have got off on the wrong foot this morning, Nick; I think we should start today all over again.' She shook her head. 'We're both tired from a disturbed night's sleep—'

'For the wrong reason—unfortunately!' he snapped scathingly, moving past her out of the doorway, brushing lightly against her before going out into the hallway and ascending the stairs two at a time on his way to his bedroom.

Gemini watched him go, a perplexed frown marring her creamy brow. What had happened to that easy, if polite friendship that had once existed between them? Because it was no longer there. It had been replaced by... She wasn't sure what it had been replaced by, but it wasn't comfortable, whatever it was.

As proved by the arousal of her nipples beneath the silk of her pyjama top! Nick had barely touched her on his way out of the room, and yet she had responded instantly to that brief touch, and still ached even now.

Tears sprang up into her eyes as she acknowledged that the situation between herself and Nick was becoming unbearable. And it had become so with the arrival of Jemima's baby...!

Damn Jemima!

'Mrs James can manage,' Nick drawled mockingly beside her in the car later that evening as they drove to have dinner with the Crawfords.

Gemini turned to him blankly, having been lost in

thought. She'd been distracted all day, if she were honest, looking for ways to return her relationship with Nick to being something she could at least feel comfortable with. Not that she'd come up with any answers, but she had decided her silence might at least not provoke the situation.

'Jessica,' Nick prompted impatiently at Gemini's blank expression. 'Mrs James seems more than capable of managing with her this evening,' he repeated tersely.

'I'm sure she'll be fine.' Gemini nodded confidently.

The housekeeper had been wonderful today, spending every moment she had free either talking to the baby or feeding and changing her. And Gemini had to admit that with two other adults in the house who obviously knew what they were doing she didn't feel so nervous about caring for Jessica herself now.

'My sister hasn't bothered to telephone yet, though, has she?' she added hardly.

And considering that Janey Reynolds, with all that she must have had to do on her wedding day, had still found the time to call in for a few minutes on her way to the hairdresser's, made the lack of even a telephone call from Jemima even more noticeable!

It really was too bad of Jemima not to have at least made sure the baby had been safely delivered to her. But that was typical Jemima; she expected everyone else to fall in with what she arranged, never dreaming for a moment that someone wouldn't do it. The thing was, she was usually right...

Nick stared grimly ahead. 'I thought we had agreed not to discuss your sister,' he bit out harshly.

They hadn't agreed any such thing, but if she wanted this evening to be anywhere near a success perhaps it would be better if they didn't! Besides, whether Jemima telephoned or not, it wouldn't make any difference to the fact

Jessica would be staying with them until her mother returned.

'Sorry,' she mumbled dismissively. 'You're looking very nice this evening,' she added lightly.

'You've seen me in a dinner suit dozens of times before,' Nick returned shortly, glancing at her with narrowed eyes.

So she had, but the fact that he looked devastatingly attractive in a black dinner suit and snowy white shirt had become more and more apparent to her in recent months! As had everything else about this man who was her husband...

He was tall and slender, with not an ounce of superfluous flesh on his body, but at the same time muscularly powerful. And his harshly hewn features—piercing green eyes, aquiline nose, sculptured lips, squarely determined jaw— were all mesmerisingly attractive.

Nick didn't just have an air of being arrogantly confident, he actually was, and women—all women, it seemed—reacted to that combination of self-confidence and good looks. Including Gemini!

Why hadn't she been aware of all these things before she married him? If she had been she might not have accepted his proposal! But the truth of the matter was at the time Nick had been Jemima's fiancé, and so of no romantic interest to Gemini. And, of course, there had been Danny...

After being with Nick over a year, and having come to know and appreciate his quiet strength and success, she couldn't understand how she'd ever found his reprehensible younger brother of any interest whatsoever.

Novelty, probably, she'd finally decided. Whatever it was, time had shown her that the infatuation—because that was exactly what it had been!—would never have lasted. Involved in the world of fashion as she was, Gemini had glamour and excitement in her life already, but she also liked a certain amount of structure, and Danny hadn't had any of that in his life, had never intended having any, either.

'You don't have to make polite conversation with me, Gemini,' Nick rasped at her lengthy silence following his earlier remark.

'But—' Gemini bit off her protest; what was the point in telling him there had been nothing polite about her comment, that she really did find him heart-stoppingly attractive in the dark evening clothes? None whatsoever, she assured herself; she'd already made enough an idiot of herself for one weekend.

'Whereas I can safely tell you that you look absolutely stunning this evening,' he added with dry mockery.

Her brows rose. 'Double standards, Nick?'

He shrugged. 'I don't think so. A dinner suit on a man rarely looks any different from the first time a woman sees him in it, whereas a woman can wear any number of different outfits for the same occasions. And that blue shimmering dress is the exact colour of your eyes; you look wonderful!'

'Thank you,' Gemini accepted, deciding to leave the conversation on that positive note and relaxing back in her car seat, wallowing in Nick's compliment.

She hoped that last part of their conversation would set the tone for the evening ahead, and both of them were relaxed as they arrived at their hosts' home, chatting easily as they lounged in the sitting-room with the elderly couple before dinner.

John Crawford was a business acquaintance of Nick's, and his wife Mary an extremely welcoming hostess, and whether or not it was because both Gemini and Nick were parentless themselves Gemini wasn't sure, but they both got along with the elderly couple in a pleasantly relaxed way.

John and Mary were more than usually talkative this evening, having returned from a holiday in Florida several days earlier.

'I love the golf out there,' John confided happily.

'And I love the food.' Mary looked down pointedly at her rounded but curvaceous figure. 'Are the two of you planning any holidays shortly?' she enquired interestedly.

Gemini and Nick didn't plan holidays—for the simple reason they never went away anywhere together! Nick had his business trips, as did she, and the suggestion of them going away together had never come up. She'd never thought about it before, but Gemini realised now that fact probably appeared a little odd to friends like John and Mary...

She looked to Nick, as he sat beside her on the sofa, to make a suitable reply to the question.

'As I recall,' John put in teasingly, brown eyes twinkling merrily, 'the two of you never went away on honeymoon!'

Because in their case there had been no reason for one! They had married in the morning, with Nick returning to work in his office in the afternoon while Gemini moved her things into the house. It had been efficiently, if not romantically, carried out!

'Nick was far too busy to spare the time,' Gemini dismissed lightly.

'Not too busy for a honeymoon, surely?' Mary said affectionately.

What was wrong with everyone this weekend? Gemini wondered irritably. Suddenly, it seemed to her, their private life had come under the spotlight. And she wasn't at all comfortable with it.

'Every day is a honeymoon for us, isn't it, Gemini?' Nick murmured huskily, reaching across to grasp her hand in his.

A little too painfully, it seemed to Gemini! 'It certainly is,' she murmured lightly, turning her own hand so that she might clasp his in return—at the same time briefly digging one of her nails into his palm!

But to give him his due, apart from a slight flicker of his eyes, he didn't show any reaction to the move. In fact, his hand tightened about hers, lightly crushing her fingers.

'I still think the two of you should have a honeymoon.' John frowned. 'Mary and I were married not long after the war, when money and time were tight, so we didn't have the chance of one, but it's something we've always regretted. Isn't it, my dear?' He turned to look at his wife affectionately.

Mary nodded. 'And before you know it there will be children on the way, and then no chance to be off on your own.'

Gemini pulled her hand abruptly away from Nick's, uncaring now if it should annoy him. 'That's years away yet.' She smiled at Mary to take any sting out of her words.

'Gemini has been too busy with her own career for us to think about having children,' Nick put in brusquely.

'And Nick is away from home so much, anyway,' she couldn't resist adding. 'Besides,' she continued hastily as he frowned across at her darkly, 'we have my sister's baby daughter staying with us at the moment—which will probably put us off ever having children of our own!' Gemini had meant to defuse the subject, but she could see by the sudden interest in the older couple's faces that she had done the opposite! And Nick looked positively furious at her talk of the baby.

Or was it the mention of her sister that bothered him...?

'How lovely!' Mary said excitedly. 'You must tell us all about her,' she prompted warmly.

Doting grandparents themselves, to five grandchildren, Mary and John were extremely interested to hear about

Jessica. Indeed, the conversation about the baby continued even after they had all gone through to the dining-room.

Nick's expression became blacker and blacker as the conversation went on, his prolonged silence evidence of his disapproval.

But the conversation did eventually move on to other things, and the subject of the two of them having a honeymoon had thankfully been forgotten by this time.

Nevertheless, Gemini was deeply aware of the continued grimness of Nick's mood as the evening progressed. So much so that by the time the two of them left, several hours later, Gemini wasn't at all looking forward to the drive home alone in the car with him.

But Nick was surprisingly silent in the dark quietness of the car, driving with his usual competence—until Gemini couldn't stand the silence any longer.

'Just say what you have to say, Nick, and get it over with!' she told him agitatedly. 'I feel like a naughty little girl sitting here waiting for chastisement!' she added disgustedly.

He glanced at her, a glimmer of amusement showing on his harsh features in the light given off by the street-lamps that lined the road they drove down. 'The sort of chastisement I would like to administer couldn't possibly be carried out in a moving car—especially as I'm the one driving it!' he finally drawled wryly.

Gemini looked at him sharply; what on earth did he mean?

'Why the hell have you never said you would have liked to have gone away on honeymoon?' he suddenly rasped, that humour of a few moments ago quickly evaporating.

She swallowed hard, frowning. That wasn't what she'd said earlier—was it...? She couldn't remember exactly what she *had* said now. Besides, that wasn't the part of the conversation that had upset Nick!

'Stop changing the subject, Nick,' she snapped impatiently. 'We both know that isn't why you're so annoyed with me.'

'Do we?' His tone was mild—too mild.

But the last twenty-four hours had been some of the most difficult Gemini had had to deal with in their marriage, and she wasn't in the mood for word games. 'I only mentioned Jessica earlier as a way of distracting John and Mary's attention away from our relationship—or lack of it!' she defended, her blue eyes flashing her irritation.

'Well, you certainly succeeded,' Nick drawled sarcastically. 'An evening talking about babies—especially other people's!—is not my idea of relaxation!'

Her cheeks burnt hotly. 'Why don't you say it, Nick? An evening talking about *Jemima's* baby isn't your idea of relaxation!' Her eyes glowed angrily across at him in the gloom.

'As it happens—no, it damn well isn't!' he acknowledged harshly. 'Your sister is one of the most irresponsible women I have ever had the misfortune to meet; the last thing I want is for people to imagine you are in the least like her!'

And yet he had loved Jemima. And he didn't seem to love her...

'Or to know that you were once engaged to marry her,' Gemini reminded him, desperately trying to keep control of the hurt that was welling up inside. It would be positively the last straw if she were to burst into tears! 'And you have no need to worry on my account, Nick,' she assured him bleakly. 'I'll never let you down as your social hostess again.'

He gave her an impatient glance. 'I never said you had let me down, damn it,' he rasped. 'Only that the conversation this evening left a lot to be desired.'

'John and Mary seemed quite happy with it,' she said

dully, knowing that she was very close to letting those un-wanted tears fall.

It had all just been too much since Jessica's arrival in their life the evening before. It wouldn't have been so bad if Nick had continued to stay away on business.

Damn it, she usually couldn't wait for him to return home, and now she was cursing the fact that this time he had come home too soon!

Nick gave a heavy sigh. 'I think the best thing to do about this evening is to just forget it ever happened,' he snapped. 'Except for one part of it, it's been a very for-gettable evening,' he added grimly.

Gemini looked at him warily, blinking back the tears. 'And which part would that be?'

'Stay and have a nightcap with me when we get in, Gemini.' Nick reached out and briefly squeezed her hand in his before returning his hand to the steering-wheel. 'I think there are some things we need to talk about.'

She swallowed hard. Things they needed to talk about...? Such as what?

Thirty-six hours ago Gemini had known exactly who she was, and hopefully where she was going. She was Gemini Stone, founder of GemStone, a fashion label that was fast making a name for itself. She was also the wife of Nick Drummond. Maybe in name only, but she had felt secure and cared for, if not loved, as Nick's wife.

But now Jessica, and necessarily her mother, Jemima, had entered that well-ordered existence, rocking the very foundations of Gemini's life and, most especially, her mar-riage to Nick.

Was that why Nick wanted to talk to her? Had Jessica's arrival in their lives, such a tangible reminder of Jemima, made him realise that their emotionless marriage wasn't what he wanted after all?

Was this going to be it? The time when Nick told her

that their marriage wasn't what he wanted? Oh, God, she couldn't bear it if it was!

But she wouldn't have any choice... Theirs was a business marriage, and, like all business contracts, it could be terminated if one side wasn't happy with the terms and conditions.

Gemini sank back in the leather car seat. 'If that's what you want, Nick,' she agreed wearily.

He sighed. 'I'm not sure I can have what I want, Gemini—I think that's one of the things we have to talk about.'

He did want to end their marriage!

And, loving him as she did, how was she going to be able to bear it?

CHAPTER FOUR

Mrs James was in the kitchen preparing a feed for Jessica when they got in. The baby was wide awake as she sat in her bouncy chair, gurgling merrily to herself as she waited patiently for her food to appear.

A vast improvement on the desperation with which she had demanded her bottle the previous evening, Gemini acknowledged wryly. But they were all more familiar with each other now, and the baby obviously felt much more secure in her new environment.

Something Gemini no longer felt at all!

'Let me do that,' she offered to the housekeeper, putting her evening bag down on the kitchen table. 'You've had a long day, and I'm sure you'd like to get to bed.' Anything to delay the moment when she and Nick had their 'talk'!

'Yes, you get to bed, Mrs James,' Nick encouraged, having quietly entered the kitchen behind Gemini. 'I'm sure Gemini and I can manage now.'

Which told Gemini very clearly that Nick wasn't going to be put off from having their talk by her delaying tactic in offering to feed the baby!

'Well...if you're sure?' Rachel James accepted lightly, wiping her hands on a towel after preparing the bottle. 'Jessica has been a little darling all evening,' she added with an indulgent smile at her young charge. 'Did the two of you have a nice time?' she asked with polite interest.

'It was—pleasant.' Nick was the one to answer her dryly. 'Perhaps you would like to go and change before feeding the baby, Gemini?' He turned to her. 'You wouldn't want to ruin that beautiful gown by getting milk all down it.'

51

No, she wouldn't—but she didn't intend talking to Nick in her nightclothes again, either; she'd feel at a distinct disadvantage before the conversation even began!

'I'll be fine,' she dismissed coolly, picking up the baby— only to nearly drop her at Mrs James's next remark!

'Oh, I almost forgot—there was a telephone call for you earlier, Mrs Drummond.' The housekeeper stopped on her way out of the kitchen.

Jemima! So her irresponsible sister had finally got round to checking up on her baby daughter. And not before time, either! Although, from the grimness of his expression, Nick had also guessed who the call had been from—and he wasn't at all pleased about Jemima telephoning here! Or at least at not being here to take the call himself...

Well, Gemini couldn't say she was too happy with the idea of her sister telephoning here whenever she felt like it, but at the moment they really didn't have any choice in the matter. 'Yes?' she prompted anxiously.

The housekeeper looked a little uncomfortable herself now, as if she weren't quite sure what to say next.

Of course, Rachel James had worked for Nick for ten years now, would know that Nick had once been engaged to marry her sister, Jemima!

That fact had never really occurred to Gemini before, but she could see now that the older woman must find this situation more than a little strange. Was it any wonder!

'It's all right, Rachel,' she encouraged understandingly. 'I've been expecting the call.'

The housekeeper looked relieved. 'That's all right, then.' She brightened. 'Of course, I explained to Mr Daniel that the two of you were out for the evening, but—'

'Mr Daniel?' Nick cut in harshly. 'Are you saying that it was my brother who rang here this evening?' He watched the housekeeper with narrowed, glittering green eyes.

Danny...!

What on earth…?

'And he wanted to speak to Gemini?' Nick added coldly, giving Gemini an accusing look.

Gemini was shaken herself by the fact that Danny had been the caller and not Jemima, after all. But Nick's re-action to it was even more disturbing than the call itself! Exactly what thoughts were going through his coldly de-cisive mind…?

She knew what her own were: why on earth was Danny telephoning here at all, let alone asking to speak to her?

Not only had she not spoken to Jemima in over a year, but she hadn't seen or spoken to Danny, either. After she'd found him and Jemima together, and the two of them had admitted they were in a relationship, there had been nothing left for Gemini and Danny to say to each other.

She chanced another glance at Nick. She could tell by his coldly harsh expression that he was absolutely furious. And not just at Danny…

She turned to smile reassuringly at the housekeeper. 'Did—Mr Daniel say why he was calling?' she prompted casually—because she couldn't think of a single reason why Danny would want to speak to her!

'No.' Rachel James grimaced. 'He did say he would call back, though,' she added reluctantly, obviously sensing some of the tense atmosphere that now existed in the kitchen.

Most of it was coming from Nick! He stood broodingly across the kitchen from Gemini, his eyes still glittering brightly green, the grimness of his expression enough to make a lesser woman turn tail and run. Except Gemini wasn't a lesser woman!

Admittedly, her relationship with Nick seemed to have become very rocky the last twenty-four hours, to such an extent that she feared for its future. But she wasn't about to give up her marriage without a fight—in spite of Jemima's, and now Danny's, sudden intrusion!

Over a year without hearing a single word from either of them, and then within twenty-four hours she had been contacted by both of them!

'Thank you, Mrs James.' She smiled dismissively at the housekeeper. 'I'm sure we can manage now.'

Much as she would have preferred the other woman to stay, and so stall her talk with Nick, she knew she couldn't do that to the other woman. Besides, there was no guarantee that the presence of a third party would prevent Nick saying exactly what he wanted to say!

Gemini busied herself with the baby for the next couple of minutes after the housekeeper had gone to her rooms at the back of the house. She made herself comfortable in a kitchen chair, with Jessica on her knee, and began to give her the bottle of milk. It wasn't that she was completely unaware of Nick in the room with her, because it would be impossible not to feel that brooding anger eminating from him. She just chose, for the moment, to ignore him.

Why was Danny telephoning her? She didn't have any idea. And she knew that was exactly what Nick was going to demand to know!

Nick finally spoke softly. 'So my brother telephoned you this evening.'

Too softly, Gemini decided with a frown. Nick was furious, and probably with good cause, but she didn't see why that anger should be directed at her; she wasn't answerable for who Danny chose to call...

She nodded coolly. 'So it would appear.'

'A call you were "expecting",' Nick added gratingly.

Gemini frowned. Of course she hadn't been expecting a call from Danny! 'I thought it was Jemima who'd called,' she defended as she remembered telling Mrs James she'd been expecting the call.

'Did you?' Nick scorned, beginning to pace up and down the kitchen, his hands in his trouser pockets. Although his narrowed gazed remained steadily fixed on Gemini.

She frowned across at him. 'Of course I— Exactly what are you trying to imply, Nick?' she prompted, and she suddenly thought she *knew* what he was implying—and couldn't believe it!

She had left Danny in no doubt as to her disgust with him fifteen months ago, or the fact that she never wanted to speak to him again. Nick couldn't now be saying that he believed she'd done a lot more than speak to his brother during the last fifteen months—could he...? In the circumstances—namely his own phone call with Jemima the day before yesterday—she found that assumption more than a little unfair. Or could it be Nick's own guilty conscience where Jemima was concerned that had prompted the accusation...?

Nick's mouth twisted scornfully. 'It would appear my returning early from this business trip was a little inconvenient for you—and Danny!' he bit out harshly.

Gemini gasped. He *did* believe she had become involved with Danny again! 'You're being ridiculous, Nick—'

'Am I?' He cut coldly across her indignation, shaking his head. 'You said it yourself last night; you weren't expecting me back home just yet. And now, this evening, my little brother telephones you. How long has Danny been telephoning you when I'm not around, Gemini?' he demanded, his jaw clenched, his lips barely moving.

Gemini felt nauseous, her face very white beneath her make-up. Nick was right; it did look more than a little odd that Danny should have telephoned her when Nick wasn't supposed to be at home. But that didn't mean anything!

'Danny has never telephoned me here before,' she gasped emotionally. 'Whether you are or aren't at home!' This whole thing was turning into a nightmare; her calm existence of two days ago seemed like a dream—or a mirage!

Perhaps she'd just been living in a fool's paradise for the last year; especially over the last few months, when she'd begun to hope that one day Nick might begin to care for her in the same way she cared for him... And Nick believing she had become involved with Danny again was not going to help the situation!

'He usually telephones you at the salon, is that it?' Nick scorned accusingly.

'He doesn't "usually" telephone me anywhere!' she refuted indignantly. She went to her salon in town during the week to work, not to receive illicit telephone calls from other men! 'Nick.' She drew in several calming breaths; it wasn't going to help anyone if she lost her temper too! 'Whatever you may think to the contrary, I'm as surprised as you are that Danny telephoned me this evening.' She returned his gaze with unblinking blue eyes.

He came to an abrupt halt in front of her, looking down at her broodingly for several long, seemingly timeless minutes. 'I wish I could believe you,' he finally sighed. 'But—'

'But what?' she snapped, feeling as if she had a lead weight in her chest where her heart should be. 'What have I ever done to give you reason to make these accusations to me?' She cursed herself as her voice broke emotionally. 'Haven't I fulfilled my part of our marriage bargain?' she added heavily.

'To the letter,' he acknowledged grimly.

'Then—'

'I don't have reason for complaint?' he finished dryly.

And erroneously.

Gemini had been going to say something quite different. But perhaps, in the circumstances, it would be better if she kept those feelings to herself!

'I wasn't going to complain, Gemini,' Nick continued hardily. 'I just don't consider my brother a suitable lover for you!—it was his betrayal that provoked you into marrying me in the first place!'

Much better kept to herself, she decided numbly as she looked up at him dazedly. Just who *would* he consider a suitable lover for her? More to the point, who did he consider a suitable lover for himself...?

Gemini was glad at that moment of the diversion of the baby moving restlessly in her arms. She turned her attention to Jessica, her lashes lowered, hiding the sudden tears that had sprung up into her eyes.

What could she say to Nick that would convince him she wasn't involved with Danny or any other man, that *he* was the only man she wanted to be involved with? There was only one way she would be able to do that, after this recent conversation, and she couldn't do it. To tell Nick how she felt about him, after the things he had just said to her, would just leave her wide open to further pain. And humiliation...

She stood up abruptly, Jessica cradled in her arms. 'I'll bear your advice in mind,' she told Nick scathingly. 'Now I think it's time I changed the baby and got her back into bed,' she added pointedly.

There had been enough said for one night—more than enough, in Gemini's opinion—and the sooner she put an end to it the better. Whatever else Nick had wanted to say to her this evening would just have to wait; she certainly couldn't take any more of his insults and accusations at the moment!

Nick nodded tersely. 'We can continue this discussion in the morning.'

Not if she had anything to do with it, Gemini decided firmly as she changed Jessica before putting her back in her cot, lingering for several minutes to gaze down at the sleeping baby. Jessica was so beautiful, her long lashes fanning across her cheeks, her skin so soft and delicate, her little rosebud of a mouth pouting as if she was still sucking on her bottle.

It must be wonderful to be so new and untouched, Gemini decided enviously as she walked slowly down the hallway to her own bedroom, to know nothing of the pain of loving and not being loved in return.

How could Nick believe she was involved with his brother? She bridled angrily a few minutes later as, having cleansed her face and changed into her silk pyjamas, she sat in front of her mirror brushing her hair.

Okay, so Danny had telephoned here, had asked to speak to her, but that didn't prove she was having an affair with him! What it did prove was that Danny was still as insensitive and selfish as he'd always been. He had to have known his call here would not be welcomed, by Nick as much as Gemini!

The trouble with Danny, as with Jemima, was that as younger siblings—Jemima only by minutes, admittedly—they had been over-indulged, their every whim granted. Gemini knew she'd always given in to her twin, and Nick as the elder brother by ten years, had been responsible for Danny ever since Danny was only sixteen, when their parents had been killed in a car accident. How could she and Nick ever hope, after contributing to that indulgence, that their siblings would ever feel any responsibility to anyone but themselves? Wasn't Jemima's recent behaviour—leaving Jessica in the way that she had proof of that?

She would just have to hope—

Her hand was arrested in mid-brushstroke as a knock sounded on her bedroom door, and she gave a startled look in the mirror as she gazed at the door's reflection there.

Nick!

It had to be. There was a communicating door between

their two bedrooms, but it was a door that was never used, by either of them. For Gemini ever to have done so would have implied an intimacy between them that just didn't exist!

She stood up slowly, pulling on her robe as she walked to the door, her hesitation evidence of her reluctance to face yet another confrontation with Nick this evening. She already felt emotionally battered, and had been looking forward to a few minutes' respite before falling asleep. She'd thought Nick felt the same way, but obviously he'd changed his mind about postponing the rest of their conversation until morning!

Her heart was pounding erratically by the time she reached the door, and she slowly turned the handle to open it, her expression guarded.

'Mrs James!' she greeted in relief as she saw it was the other woman who stood outside in the hallway, even able to smile now that she knew her visitor wasn't Nick, after all. 'What can I do for you?' she prompted lightly.

'I just wanted to apologise in case I may have caused some—difficulty between you and Mr Drummond earlier.' The housekeeper looked worried. She was still wearing the clothes she had had on earlier, obviously not having been to bed yet, despite having left them over half an hour earlier.

'Difficulty?' Gemini forced her own voice to sound light.

Gemini didn't think Nick would thank her for letting Mrs James become aware that there was any tension between the two of them. And, in truth, she was of the same opinion herself; she didn't welcome any third party, no matter how well-meaning, knowing there was a rapidly widening rift between Nick and herself.

'I know that Mr Drummond and his brother haven't been on speaking terms since—well, that they haven't communicated with each other for some time.' Mrs James looked uncomfortable with the conversation herself, but had obviously felt the need to say something. 'And the last thing I would want to do is cause any problems between Mr Drummond and yourself,' she continued worriedly. 'I just didn't know what to do about Mr Daniel's telephone call.'

Gemini reached out and squeezed the other woman's arm reassuringly. 'You did exactly the right thing, Rachel.' She smiled.

Although she didn't feel much like smiling! Obviously Rachel James *was* aware of Nick's engagement to Jemima—*and* of Danny and Gemini's affair. And her concern now, over Danny's telephone call to Gemini, probably meant she was also aware that Gemini had been involved with Danny at the time, too. To the housekeeper's credit, she had never, by so much as a word, revealed that she was aware of the complications that had preceded Gemini and Nick's marriage...!

'If you're sure...?' The housekeeper looked unconvinced.

'I—'

'She's sure, Rachel,' Nick cut in dryly, coming to stand behind Gemini. 'In fact, we're both sure!'

Gemini gasped in surprise to find him there. He had to have used the connecting door to come into her bedroom! Not that she'd been aware of it, but there was no other way he could have entered the room without the two women having been aware of it. So much for thinking earlier that neither of them ever used that connecting door!

How much of their conversation had he overheard? More to the point, what was he doing in her bedroom at all? The black robe he wore over his nakedness showed he'd probably already been to bed before coming in here.

'I'm so sorry if I've disturbed you, Mr Drummond.' The housekeeper looked completely flustered now, an embarrassed flush to her cheeks.

'Not at all, Mrs James,' he drawled dryly, moving to put one of his arms about Gemini's waist. 'Although with a baby in the house I think it's time we all got to bed—don't you...?' he added pointedly.

Gemini was very aware of the heat of that arm about her, of the curve of Nick's hand on her waist. As far as she could remember he had never touched her so intimately before, and the fact that he did so now filled her with aching longing.

'Of course,' the housekeeper agreed rapidly, looking much relieved to see the two of them so at ease together. 'I wish you both goodnight.'

Nick was the one to move and close the door once the other woman had gone, his expression grim as he turned back to Gemini. 'What the hell was all that about?' he rasped impatiently, moving restlessly about the room.

Gemini found it disturbing to see him in the femininity of her bedroom, although he didn't look out of place in his black robe amongst the gold and cream decor. Just disturbing...

But she mustn't let the unaccustomed intimacy of this situation throw her; she knew she always needed to be one hundred per cent aware when dealing with Nick. 'I thought that communicating door was locked.' She frowned across to where the door stood slightly ajar.

Nick gave a slight inclination of his head. 'Like any sensible husband, I have the key,' he drawled mockingly.

She had wondered where it was! Well, now she knew. And Nick wasn't averse to using it when he felt the need.

'So it would appear,' she returned coolly, moving away from him. 'To what do I owe the honour of this—visit?' She deliberately hesitated over the last word. Because his presence here was an intrusion—and she intended he should know what it was.

Nick looked unperturbed by her coolness. 'I heard voices.' He shrugged. 'I decided to investigate.'

Gemini looked at him assessingly for several seconds, her smile, when it came, completely lacking in humour. 'Did you think I had sneaked down after everyone else was in bed and brought a man up to my bedroom?' she scorned hardily. She was furious to think that might be what he had imagined, what had compelled him to unlock that communicating door and come into her bedroom unannounced.

Prior to Danny there had been several men in her life, but none of them had been serious, and even Danny hadn't made her feel the way Nick did—the way she was feeling right now! She just wanted to forget the anger between them, to lose herself in the warmth of his arms, to revel in the pleasure they could give each other...

He shrugged again. 'It wouldn't have done you much good if you had!' he bit out harshly, eyes narrowed dangerously.

Gemini stood her ground, tilting her head back in challenge. 'Oh?'

Nick took a step towards her. 'I don't share, Gemini,' he grated roughly, his next step forward bringing him to within inches of touching her.

He was so close to her now that Gemini could feel the heat emanating from his body, see the faint shadow of his stubble on the squareness of his chin, smell the masculine tang of his aftershave. In fact, she was aware of everything about him!

She had to put some distance between them, if not physically, then emotionally! 'You did once before,' she reminded him pointedly, instantly regretting the defiance as Nick's expression darkened coldly.

'All the more reason why I never will again!' he bit out, reaching out to pull her roughly into his arms.

Not like this, she cried inwardly, even as Nick's mouth

came crushingly down on her own. But her body thought otherwise, her lips opening beneath his, her body melting into his hardness as he curved her ruthlessly against him.

She felt like a woman who had been on the point of drowning and had been thrown a life-raft, her hands clinging about his waist, her lips moving provocatively against his, deepening the caress as his tongue tasted, and then plunged into the warm moisture of her mouth.

He felt so good, his body firm beneath her touch, all hard muscle, the throbbing heat of his thighs telling her of his own arousal even as his lips left hers to burn a trail of fire down the column of her throat and into the hollows below.

Gemini gasped as Nick gently moved aside the restriction of her top, that questing mouth seeking, and finding, the pertness of her breast, his tongue moving silkily over her nipple in rhythmic pleasure.

Her back arched in surrender as she offered herself up to that pleasure. One of Nick's hands was caressing her other breast, and her knees felt suddenly weak as burning heat coursed through her whole body. She offered no resistance as Nick swung her up in his arms and carried her towards the bed.

She wanted this, wanted Nick. She'd wanted him for so long now she couldn't remember a time when she hadn't been completely aware of him. Nick was everything she'd ever wanted in a man. Everything...! He was—

Dropping her!

She landed on the bed from a height of about three feet, bouncing back up only to fall back down again before settling in the middle of the gold-coloured duvet, looking up at Nick with disbelieving eyes.

His expression was grim as he returned that look. The darkness of his hair was tousled from her caressing fingers, but otherwise he looked unmoved by the explosion of passion they had just shared.

Shared…?

Gemini winced at the look of cold deliberation on Nick's face, knowing as she did so that she'd been the one to be aroused seconds ago, that Nick had known exactly what he was doing.

But why?

The answer to that was all too obvious: Nick didn't share, and never, ever again with his brother. And now, after Danny's telephone call this evening, Nick believed Gemini to be once more involved with Danny…!

She drew in a deep, controlling breath, rolling over onto her side, forcing her expression to become bland as she leant on her elbow looking up at Nick. 'You're so right to be sensible, Nick,' she drawled mockingly. 'Our going to bed together at this late date in our marriage will only complicate things when it comes to the divorce!'

There, she had said the hated word, the word she had dreaded hearing from Nick all evening! And it hurt just as badly that she was the one who had finally said it!

Nick looked so angry Gemini had to force herself not to flinch from that cold fury, to maintain that nonchalant pose on the bed as she continued to look up at him dismissively.

'Divorce?' he finally echoed in that dangerously soft voice Gemini was quickly learning to be wary of. 'Oh, no, Gemini.' He shook his head, moving to kneel on the bed beside her. 'There isn't going to be any convenient divorce so that you can then marry my little brother!' he grated, pulling her up so that their faces were only inches apart.

Gemini hardly breathed as she looked at him, green eyes locked with blue in a battle of wills, a battle that seemed to go on for ever. Gemini wanted to turn away, but she didn't dare; she knew that to do so would bring an inequality between Nick and herself that would be the end of whatever relationship they did have.

Whatever that relationship was…

Gemini wasn't sure any more!

She swallowed hard. 'I don't want to marry Danny, Nick—'

He gave a harsh laugh. 'That's probably as well, because I doubt my little brother is the marrying kind.'

'It isn't that,' she gasped. 'I—'

'If you have any sense, Gemini,' he continued grimly, 'you'll hold out for the wedding ring from him this time. But in the meantime you still have to get past the problem of your marriage to me. And I can tell you now—there will be no divorce between us, Gemini,' he repeated harshly, thrusting her away from him before standing up. 'I've never given you grounds to divorce me, and I refuse ever to agree to divorce you,' he told her coldly. 'Maybe you'd better tell Danny that when he rings back!' Nick bit out contemptuously, turning to stride over to the connecting door between their two bedrooms. 'In the meantime—' he turned briefly, his green eyes icy '—there will be no more locked doors between us!' The slamming of the door behind him, unaccompanied by the turning of the key in the lock, told her exactly what he meant by that last remark.

Gemini couldn't have moved even if she'd needed to; she was totally stunned by this latest exchange between Nick and herself.

And the most important thing to come out of the conversation was that Nick didn't want to divorce her! Admittedly, it was because he believed she would go straight to his brother Danny's arms if he did, but at the moment his reasoning wasn't important, only the fact that he would never divorce her.

And if Nick were to be believed then he hadn't been involved with anyone else since their marriage, had never given her grounds to divorce him, either. It seemed incredible—wonderful!—to her, but if Nick claimed it to be the truth, then she believed him. Maybe because she wanted to believe him. But, whatever the reason, her marriage had been given a reprieve, and at the moment that was the most important thing to her.

She looked across at the connecting door. If he meant what she thought he did where that unlocked door was concerned, then he was going to find he didn't have a fight on his hands. She was more than willing to be his wife. Completely.

The only uncertainty she had about it was when would it happen…?

CHAPTER FIVE

BREAKFAST the next morning, despite the presence of the gurgling Jessica, was a very quiet affair. Nick ate in stony silence, and Gemini was unwilling to break that silence.

Because she didn't know what to say! Everything, it seemed, had been said the previous evening. Now it was a question of waiting to see what happened next.

But it certainly wasn't the time for Mrs James to quietly enter the room and tell her that Danny was on the telephone again!

Gemini looked uncertainly at Nick, not at all encouraged by his grim expression as he met her gaze over the rim of the coffee cup he held. But at least the coffee stayed in the cup and wasn't thrown over her, she decided ruefully.

He straightened, carefully replacing the cup on its saucer. 'Tell him Mrs Drummond will take his call in a moment,' he instructed the housekeeper tersely, waiting until she'd left the room before turning back to Gemini. 'Remember what I said last night, Gemini,' he bit out tautly. 'I suggest you also remember what happened fifteen months ago,' he added scornfully.

She was hardly likely ever to forget that past humiliation. But, as Nick had said the previous evening, Danny's affair with Jemima was also the reason she was now married to Nick, and in retrospect she knew that was the best thing that could ever have happened to her!

'I haven't forgotten, Nick,' she assured him dryly.

He nodded abruptly. 'Take the call in the sitting-room; I have no wish to overhear even your end of the conversation!' he added disgustedly.

Gemini stood up slowly, glancing uncertainly at the baby where she lay contentedly in her bouncy chair beside the table. Maybe she was getting used to it, Gemini decided, or she just hadn't felt too much in need of sleep, but getting up to feed the baby in the early hours of this morning hadn't seemed quite as bad as it had the night before.

She knew she was also becoming attached to the tiny, defenceless baby, that it was impossible not to love such an endearing child. In fact, in spite of the inconvenience she'd initially found in Jessica's arrival, she knew the house was going to seem very quiet and empty without her sunny presence.

'Leave her with me,' Nick barked dismissively as he saw her hesitation as she looked down at the baby. 'At this moment, Jessica is the least complicated female I know!' he added self-derisively.

With a rueful grimace, Gemini went into the adjoining sitting-room to pick up the receiver. 'Hello, Danny,' she greeted him dryly, making herself comfortable on the sofa.

'Gemini!' He sounded pleased to hear her voice at least—the reason for that becoming obvious a few seconds later! 'Where's the Big Bad Wolf?' he prompted conspiratorially, using the name he had always used when talking to her of his older brother.

It wasn't an intimacy Gemini felt in the least inclined to encourage! 'If you're referring to Nick, he's still having his breakfast,' she returned coolly.

'Of course I'm referring to Nick,' Danny came back unrepentantly. 'How is he?'

Gemini frowned. Not because of the question, but because she didn't know how to answer it. If Danny had asked her two days ago how Nick was then she would have answered that he was fine, but after the weekend—she just didn't know!

'Nick is very well,' she answered evasively; his health

appeared to be good, but she couldn't really vouch for his emotional state. And this call wasn't helping! 'Danny—'

'And you, are you well too?' Danny continued quickly.

'Very,' she assured him wryly, aware that he was using delaying tactics for what he really wanted to say. 'Why have you telephoned me, Danny?' she prompted bluntly.

He gave a softly appreciative laugh. 'I think you've been living with my big brother too long, Gemini; you're starting to sound like him!'

'It could be worse,' she came back pointedly; she might not like all that Nick had to say, especially at the moment, but at least she knew he didn't lie to her!

'You still hate me,' Danny realised heavily.

'Hate is far too strong a word for what I feel towards you, Danny,' she assured him. 'Hate, like love, is an emotion that has to be fed, nurtured, or it dies—and I don't think of you often enough to feel either emotion towards you!' In fact, she realised, until the last couple of days she hadn't given Danny a thought for months!

Because she had fallen in love with Nick! But Danny, selfish, thoughtless Danny, wouldn't understand, or believe her, if she told him she had fallen in love with her own husband!

'Does that mean you've forgiven me, at least?' Danny prompted softly.

'Forgiveness is something that has to be earned,' she told him non-committally. And in this case there was no forgiveness necessary; Danny, with Jemima as his accomplice, had probably done her the biggest favour of her life by having an affair!

Danny gave a deep sigh. 'You always were a tough lady, Gemini.'

'What do you want, Danny?' she prompted impatiently.

'If you really want to know the truth—'

'That would be a nice change—coming from you!'

'I deserved that,' Danny accepted heavily. 'I— You—'

'This hesitation isn't like you, Danny,' Gemini taunted. 'This must be serious.'

'It is,' he acknowledged. 'The thing is, Gemini, I'm trying to contact Jemima,' he told her bluntly.

Jemima...

She should have guessed, should have known Danny didn't really want to talk to *her*; there really was nothing left for them to say to each other.

But the last she'd heard of Jemima and Danny *they* hadn't had anything to say to each other, either; their relationship had only lasted a few weeks after Gemini and Nick had married each other! Not that she had any intention of asking Danny why he wanted to locate Jemima again; she simply wasn't interested in anything either of them did any more.

But how ironic this all was! Nick was sitting in the dining-room at this moment, probably imagining all sorts of things, and all the time Danny was simply trying to contact Jemima. How Nick would laugh if she were to tell him that!

'Why telephone me?' she prompted Danny coolly. 'Jemima and I haven't spoken for—sometime,' she dismissed.

'Fifteen months, to be exact—'

'Oh, let's be exact, shall we, Danny?' Gemini cut in impatiently, needing no reminder of exactly how long it was since she had discovered Danny's affair with Jemima.

'Gemini—' he began apologetically.

'I can't help you with locating Jemima, Danny,' she continued. 'For the simple reason I have no idea where she is.' If she did, she would have contacted her sister herself by now! 'Have you tried telephoning her?'

'Of course I've—! Sorry,' Danny muttered awkwardly after his angry outburst. 'I have telephoned her, and she's not at the apartment. I didn't know where else to try...'

'I'm the last resort, hmmm?' Gemini acknowledged dryly. 'Well, I'm sorry to disappoint you, Danny, but I haven't heard from Jemima, either.' Jemima instructing her nanny to deliver her young daughter here did not constitute having heard from her in Gemini's book!

'Damn,' Danny grumbled under his breath. 'I'm at a complete loss who to try next.'

'Have you tried the newspaper she works for—?'

'Jemima works freelance now,' Danny cut in dismissively. 'Damn it, she could be anywhere!'

'She's a big girl, Danny.' Gemini shrugged, inwardly surprised that he knew so much about her sister's movements. The last Gemini had heard, the two of them had gone their separate ways. 'But if you do manage to find her, have her give me a call, will you?' she added briskly. 'There's something I need to talk to her about.'

'Sure,' Danny agreed distractedly. 'I'm really sorry to have bothered you, Gemini.'

'It was no bother,' she assured him dryly.

'Say hello to Nick for me, will you?' he added hopefully.

'Why don't you say hello to him yourself?' she came back impatiently.

'You know why,' he muttered. 'Obviously you don't bear a grudge, but Nick certainly does!'

Because Danny had taken the woman Nick had loved and had intended to marry! But Nick was married to her now, for better or for worse, and it was time all of this stopped—past time, as far as she was concerned.

'You'll never know whether or not that's still true if you don't speak to him,' she pointed out practically.

'I'll take a raincheck, if you don't mind.' The grimace could be heard in his voice. 'Sorry to have bothered you, Gemini. And thanks for your help,' he added abruptly before ringing off.

Gemini slowly put down her own receiver. She hadn't

been of any help to Danny, and they both knew it. Nor did she have any idea why Danny was trying to contact Jemima. But she knew that the two of them had worked together a couple of times during their three-month relationship, so maybe it had something to do with that...?

Whatever, she had more important things to think about than either Danny or her sister.

Nick, for one.

For two...

And for three!

What was she going to tell him about this telephone call? Because she would have to tell him something. But he probably wouldn't believe a word she said anyway!

Nick looked up from playing with the baby as Gemini came back into the dining-room. His gaze narrowed on her questioningly but he didn't say a word, not as she poured herself a fresh cup of coffee or when she sat down opposite him at the table again.

Gemini gave him a bright, meaningless smile. 'Danny said to say hello,' she informed him lightly.

Nick raised dark brows. 'Am I supposed to be impressed?' he drawled scathingly.

She shrugged. 'I did tell him I thought he should speak to you himself, but he didn't seem too sure of his reception.'

Nick's mouth twisted. 'I wonder why!'

'I—'

'What else did he want, Gemini?' Nick rasped impatiently, obviously tired of waiting for her to give him an explanation of his brother's telephone call.

Afraid of Nick's reaction, she cowardly began with the rest of Danny's conversation, rather than his main point. 'He just seemed to want a general chat,' she dismissed, meeting Nick's accusing gaze with a challenge of her own.

'He asked me how everyone was. Including Jemima,' she added pointedly.

'He could have spoken to me for that,' Nick scorned disbelievingly.

'I just told you,' Gemini reminded him. 'He wasn't sure of your reaction.'

'My "reaction" would have been a damn sight less annoyed if he had spoken to me instead of asking to speak to my wife!' Nick grated, standing up abruptly, obviously preparing to leave the dining-room. 'What do you intend doing with the rest of today?' he prompted suspiciously.

He obviously believed she intended meeting Danny some time today! And she couldn't let him go on believing that!

She sighed. 'Nick, if you really want to know the reason Danny called—'

'I thought you had just told me the reason,' he cut in accusingly.

Prevaricating about the truth in this case was just complicating matters further.

'He's trying to find Jemima, Nick, that's the real reason he telephoned here!' she burst out reluctantly, shaking her head self-derisively. 'I was the last resort, apparently,' she added disgustedly.

'He's trying to *what*?' Nick exploded disbelievingly.

Gemini recoiled at the force of his attack. 'Find Jemima—'

'I don't believe you,' Nick scorned, shaking his head. 'Jemima would have no more interest in talking to Danny than I have!'

Gemini frowned. 'I didn't say Jemima wanted to talk to Danny, only that he wanted to find her,' she correctly softly; and since when had Nick become such an expert on what Jemima might want...? 'And I don't tell lies,' she added quietly, meeting his stormy gaze unflinchingly.

Nick looked down at her wordlessly for several long

minutes, his narrowed gaze cynically thoughtful. Finally he shook his head, his expression scornful. 'I think I found your first explanation more believable, Gemini—'

'But this happens to be the truth!' she gasped protestingly, amazed at how he had managed to turn this around onto her!

'I'm sure you know the story of the little boy and the wolf...?' he prompted dryly. 'Well, you just cried wolf once too often!' he muttered grimly at her confirming nod.

'But—'

'And now it looks as if you have Jessica to take care of.' He looked down to where the baby was starting to fidget for her next feed. 'I have some papers to deal with in my study today,' he said dismissively. 'But I'll join you for dinner this evening,' he added pointedly.

In other words, he was going to be in the house all day, and would know if she made any attempt to go out! To meet Danny, no doubt!

'Fine,' she acknowledged tightly, picking Jessica up and deliberately preceding him out of the dining-room. 'I think I'll take Jessica out for a walk in her pushchair after her feed,' she informed him definitely; she was not going to become a prisoner in her own home—no matter what Nick did or didn't believe about Danny's telephone call!

'Good idea,' Nick agreed smoothly. 'Give me a shout when you're ready to go and I'll come with you. I could do with some fresh air myself,' he added as Gemini turned sharply to look up at him.

'Fresh air be damned,' Gemini muttered to herself as she prepared the baby's feed. Nick didn't even trust her to take the baby for a walk on her own now!

This was all so silly. They had been married for fourteen months now, and during that time they'd both been away on their own—on business, of course. And never once during that time had Nick given any indication that he didn't trust her either to stay here on her own or to go away on her own. Now it seemed he didn't even trust her to go out of the house for a short walk on her own!

Besides which, they looked ridiculous walking in the park together, Gemini decided an hour or so later. She was in charge of the pushchair while Nick strolled along at her side. They looked for all the world like any other family: doting parents out walking with their young baby on a Sunday afternoon!

Gemini almost choked when Nick suggested they stop by the pond and feed the ducks, especially when he even produced some stale bread from his jacket pocket for the purpose. He took Jessica from the pushchair to crouch down with her on his knee as he gave Gemini the bread to break up and throw for the waiting birds.

Gemini couldn't believe she was doing this! It was so totally out of context with the way their marriage had been up to this point! 'Maybe the two of us should have had a baby,' Nick murmured thoughtfully.

Gemini stared down at him. What on earth—?

Nick glanced up at her. 'You like children, don't you?'

Until the last couple of days she hadn't given the question any thought. But Jessica, with her gurgling chuckles and her complete vulnerability, had somehow wriggled her way into Gemini's heart…

And why shouldn't she? Jessica was her niece, after all. But as for a baby of her own—it was something she had never even thought about!

Nick's baby…

Just the thought of having his child made her tremble. And Nick would make a wonderful father, she thought, looking at how naturally he handled Jessica.

What was she doing?

The two of them couldn't have a child for the simple reason they didn't have that sort of marriage! Or was that what Nick was saying...? That after last night that was all going to change?

'Other people's,' she confirmed abruptly. 'But a child between the two of us would really complicate matters!'

His mouth twisted wryly. 'Wouldn't it just?' he murmured mockingly, straightening to tuck Jessica into a half sitting position in the curve of his arm. 'I'll just walk her round to the other side of the pond and show her the fish,' he told Gemini dismissively.

In other words, this was a Nick and Jessica thing—so much for Gemini taking the baby for a walk! Not that Gemini minded too much, and she moved to sit down on a bench that faced the pond, her legs feeling slightly weak after their recent conversation.

A baby. Surely Nick wasn't suggesting—? No, he had said they 'should have had' a baby; the past tense.

Would things be any different between them now if they had had a normal marriage from the outset, if they had shared a bed as well as a home? Probably, she acknowledged, sadly. For wasn't all this a little late for them now...?

'Boy or girl?'

Gemini turned sharply at the sound of the voice, finding that while she had been lost in thought a young lady with a pushchair parked at her side had joined her on the bench.

'Sorry?' Gemini prompted apologetically.

The young woman, who was three or four years younger than Gemini's twenty-nine years, with flowing blonde hair and friendly blue eyes, nodded across the pond to where Nick was busy showing the baby the fish gliding in the water. 'I asked if you have a little boy or a little girl?'

Gemini's brow cleared. 'I—' She came to an abrupt halt. What was the point of going into explanations concerning Jessica's parentage—or lack of it? 'A little girl,' she supplied lightly. 'She's six weeks old.' At least she had been on Friday; not knowing the actual date of Jessica's birth, she really couldn't be more accurate than that!

'My little boy is six months old.' The young woman nodded to where the baby lay sleeping in the pushchair beside her. 'He seems to have got his clocks a bit confused at the moment, because he's awake all night and sleeps all day!' She grinned ruefully.

'Poor you,' Gemini sympathised with feeling; and she had thought *she* had problems just getting up for Jessica twice in the night!

The young woman shrugged. 'Your husband obviously adores her,' she murmured appreciatively, once again looking across the pond.

Gemini followed her gaze, her breath catching in her throat as Nick laughed at that moment at Jessica's tiny hands moving in an attempt to touch the water. Nick certainly did have a way with Jessica...

'But then,' the young woman added softly, 'she looks so much like you.'

Actually, Jessica looked very like her mother, with her dark, almost black hair and deep blue eyes, her features a tiny replica of Jemima's. Although some of Jessica must be her father—whoever he might be! But as Gemini and Jemima were physically identical twins, it wasn't surprising that this woman should think Jessica resembled Gemini...

'Yes,' she acknowledged non-committally.

'You're very lucky your husband takes such an interest in her,' the young woman said wistfully. 'Mine's off watching a football match somewhere.'

And Gemini's 'husband' was only with her at the moment because he had no intention of allowing her to go anywhere on her own where she might possibly meet the man he believed to be her lover—his own brother!

'I'm not expecting the novelty to last too long, either,' Gemini assured the other woman dryly. 'At the moment

Jessica is small and unobtrusive—I'm just waiting until she can walk and talk, then we'll see how often Nick walks in the park with us!'

The young woman laughed appreciatively as she stood up. 'I suppose I had better get back and cook the lunch. It was nice talking to you,' she added warmly before turning to walk towards one of the park exits.

Gemini continued to smile even after the woman had gone. It had been fun, just for a few brief minutes, to pretend she and Nick were Jessica's parents, to laugh and joke with someone on the subject of children and husbands.

'Who was that?' Nick rasped suspiciously.

She sighed, her smile fading as she looked up at him. 'I have no idea,' she told him truthfully.

'But the two of you were talking together,' he pointed out reasonably.

She drew in a deeply controlling breath. 'Apparently talking to each other is something that mothers do when they go to the park with their children,' she returned sarcastically, standing up to take the baby from him and put her back in her pushchair, completely ignoring Nick as she did so.

Only to find him still watching her with narrowed eyes when she straightened. For goodness' sake, who did he think the young woman was? A friend of Danny's sent to pass her a message? If he did, he was becoming jealously possessive, and somehow that role didn't sit too well with the self-confident man she was married to.

'It's probably because being tied down at home with a baby all day they have so few people to talk to!' Gemini added scathingly.

'Is that what you think motherhood is, being "tied down"?' Nick murmured quizzically.

She'd said something wrong again! But then, when did she do anything else just recently?

'Not exactly,' she answered dismissively, resuming pushing the pushchair. 'Although I'm sure that young lady does!'

Nick fell into step beside her. 'It doesn't have to be that way. There are nannies—'

'Nick, I think this nesting feeling you're exhibiting is wonderful—but sure to be fleeting!' she told him. 'Babies don't stay the size of Jessica for very long, Nick, they get bigger, and as they get bigger they get talkative, inquisitive, *mobile*—'

'Okay, okay, I get the point, Gemini,' Nick cut in impatiently. 'What you're really trying to say is that motherhood isn't for you!'

No, she wasn't saying that at all. It hadn't been, certainly, but Jessica's arrival in their lives was slowly changing that...

No!

The way things were between Nick and herself now, and with the deterioration in their relationship the last two days, there was no way she would even contemplate bringing a baby into their marriage.

'I'm a career-woman, Nick,' she told him coldly. 'You knew that when you married me.'

He quirked dark brows. 'Did I?'

'Yes!' she insisted firmly. 'Now it's your turn to push this damned thing!' She handed over the pushchair, once against shaken by the intensity of their conversation, inwardly apologising to Jessica for seeming resentful of her presence.

The truth of the matter was she was growing to love Jessica very much, was even starting to distinguish which cries meant the baby was hungry and which meant she was either bored or needed her nappy changing.

But she knew it wasn't a good idea for her to love the baby too much. When it suited her, Jemima would return, and when she did she would just take Jessica away with her.

When Jemima returned…

Although when that was going to be was anyone's guess…!

Gemini was in no way reassured, when they returned to the house a short time later, to be informed by Mrs James that Jemima had telephoned while they were out, and that she was going to be delayed in America for several more days!

And once again her irresponsible sister had refused to leave a contact telephone number!

Jemima couldn't possibly have known that both Gemini and Nick would be out of the house when she telephoned, especially on a Sunday morning, but nevertheless Gemini still felt furious at her sister's selfishness.

'Looks as if the "career-woman" will have to go on hold for a few days,' Nick drawled mockingly once the house-keeper had returned to the kitchen.

Gemini's eyes flashed brightly blue as she turned to glare at him. 'Not at all,' she bit out challengingly. 'Jessica will just have to come to the salon with me in the morning.' Until this moment she'd been nonplussed herself as to what to do with Jessica while she worked, but Nick's mockery had spurred her into defensive action.

And why not take Jessica to work with her?

What harm could it possibly do?

CHAPTER SIX

'FOR goodness' sake put the baby down for a few minutes, Hugh, and let's get some work done!' Gemini grumbled, frowning across at her assistant as he strolled about their workroom holding Jessica against one of his broad shoulders.

What harm could there be, she had thought last night, in bringing the baby to work with her? There was no real 'harm' in it; it was just that Hugh treated Jessica much as he did the spoilt cat he had at home in his flat, constantly carrying the baby, talking to her incessantly in sugar-coated baby-talk!

So much so that it wasn't even lunchtime yet, and Gemini felt nauseous!

Hugh looked across at her reprovingly. 'Shh,' he hissed softly. 'You'll wake her!'

'Babies are supposed to sleep through noise,' Gemini told him wearily.

Hugh obviously had no idea how ridiculous he looked in his new role of nursemaid—and he probably wouldn't have cared even if he did!

There was only one way to describe Hugh Pickering, with his mousse-spiked dyed blond hair, battle-scarred face and huge, powerful body; he looked like the bouncer from a particularly seedy nightclub!

But that assumption was untrue from every angle where Hugh was concerned. He was one of the gentlest men Gemini had ever met, and literally couldn't bear to harm even a fly. And the battle-scarred face had come from his teen years, when he had decided to be honest about his sexuality and had received several beatings for his candidness.

But the world of fashion was less judgemental about such things, and Hugh was a wonderful fashion assistant; he could literally take one of Gemini's designs and bring it to sensational life. The two of them had worked together for five years now, and Gemini, for one, hoped that would never change.

'Put the baby down, Hugh,' she told him patiently. 'She'll sleep far better, and probably longer too, if she's in her carrycot.'

The look on Hugh's face had been priceless this morning, when she'd staggered into the salon with Jessica in the carrycot! If she had walked in stark naked he would probably have looked less stunned. And less interested too, she acknowledged ruefully.

But it turned out that Hugh adored babies. And it was an adoration Jessica had seemed to return from the very first moment Hugh had picked her up. But after almost three hours of this mutual adoration Gemini had had enough!

'Work, Hugh,' she reminded him pointedly.

He sighed, moving to put Jessica in her carrycot as requested. 'You're very grouchy this morning, Gem,' he complained as he tucked the blankets about the baby—even the roughness of his voice sounded as if it came over sandpaper.

She wasn't grouchy, exactly, more irritable. And she knew the reason for it too!

She had been so sure on Saturday night that Nick meant to make their marriage a real one, had half expected him to come to her bedroom last night. But after reading for half an hour after they had both retired for the night, she'd had to accept that she was going to be sleeping alone, after all.

It was sheer frustration that was making her so grumpy!

She felt like a taut string ready to snap. And she wasn't sure who her target was going to be when she did!

'Don't call me Gem,' she snapped as Hugh finally left the baby and came back to the table where they had been working earlier. 'You know how much I hate it!'

Which hadn't always been the case. Gemini had never particularly minded that shortened version of her name— until she'd realised Danny had called her that because when spoken it would apply to both sisters without getting him into any trouble whichever twin he was with! Since that time she had always insisted on her full name being used, and she had noted long ago that Nick always called her Gemini—probably for the opposite reason of his brother; Nick had wanted to know exactly which twin he was with!

Hugh raised dark brows as he sat down beside her. 'Everything okay in the Drummond household?'

Gemini gave him a sharp look. 'What do you mean?'

He grimaced. 'You aren't usually moody, Gem— Gemini,' he hastily corrected. 'This morning you're a trifle...edgy?'

She sighed. 'Sorry,' she muttered. 'I'm probably just not used to having my nights disturbed—' She broke off as she saw Hugh's teasingly raised brows, colour heating her cheeks as she easily read his thoughts. 'By a baby, I meant!' she added crossly.

She and Hugh might have worked together for years, and were very good friends, but even he wasn't aware of the business arrangement of her marriage. There had never been any reason for Hugh to know; he hadn't liked Danny, but he definitely approved of Nick, and so Gemini had left Hugh his illusions concerning her marriage.

'Of course.' Hugh humoured her, holding back his teasing smile. He frowned. 'I don't suppose, in the circumstances, that Nick feels too inclined to help out.'

The circumstances being that Jessica was the daughter of Jemima, the woman who had once let Nick down so badly...

She shrugged. To give Nick his due, after his first shock at Jessica being Jemima's baby he had been more than attentive, had even taken the baby for a couple of hours yesterday afternoon so that Gemini could take a nap. No, Nick certainly hadn't passed on the resentful feelings he had towards Jemima to the baby.

'Actually, he's been very good with Jessica,' she defended. 'He—' She broke off as the door that opened onto the street was suddenly opened behind her.

'Hi, Nick,' Hugh greeted warmly as he looked over Gemini's shoulder towards the door. 'We were just talking about you!'

Gemini winced at his candidness, drawing in a controlling breath and schooling her features into polite query before turning to face Nick.

She hadn't seen him this morning, as he had breakfasted and gone out of the house before she'd come downstairs with the baby, but she could see from the formal dark suit, snowy white shirt and conservative tie that he had been to his office this morning. Why she should have thought he might have gone somewhere other than his office she didn't really know; maybe it was because their whole relationship seemed to be one big question mark at the moment!

'Something nice, I hope?' Nick drawled as he strolled further into the room, closing the door behind him, instantly shutting out the busy street noise.

The salon, as Gemini liked to call it, was really just a series of rooms in a large house that had been let for office purposes. Clothes, in different degrees of preparation, were strewn around each of the rooms as she and Hugh, along with a seamstress who came in on Thursdays and Fridays, prepared them for her next GemStone collection.

'Would I ever allow anyone to say anything nasty about you?' Hugh replied jokingly.

To Gemini's relief, the two men, so vastly different in masculinity, had got on together from their first meeting. Gemini accepted that a lot of the reason for that was probably Nick's unquestioning acceptance of who and what Hugh was. In fact Hugh and his long-term partner, Alan, often came to dinner with Gemini and Nick, when a hilarious time was usually had by all.

But at the moment, as the two men shared a moment of laughter, Gemini could well have done without the two of them getting on quite so well together!

'Did you *want* to say something nasty about me, Gemini…?' Nick looked across at her with raised brows.

She would like to say something nasty *to* him, not about him! 'As if,' she returned mockingly. 'Actually, I was just telling Hugh how wonderful you've been with the baby,' she added hastily as he saw Nick was about to pursue the subject with Hugh; the last thing she wanted was for Hugh to repeat any of that conversation about her 'disturbed' nights!

'"Very good" was the way I think Gemini put it,' Hugh put in dryly. 'Although she's such a darling I don't see how you could be anything else but good to her,' Hugh added appreciatively.

'Gemini is?' Nick drawled derisively.

The other man grinned. 'Well, of course Gemini is a darling—that goes without saying!—but I was actually referring to Jessica.'

A fact Nick was well aware of, Gemini knew! 'What can I do for you, Nick?' She cut in impatiently on their light-hearted banter; she simply wasn't in the mood for it.

Besides, Nick rarely came to the salon, and when he did it was usually because he had come to tell her he had to go away on business unexpectedly. The thought of him going away again at the moment, with everything feeling so—so unfinished between them, was unacceptable to her...

He looked at her with unfathomable green eyes. 'I called in to see if you were free for lunch,' he finally murmured softly.

Gemini's eyes widened at the invitation. Lunch? Nick never took her out for lunch! At least, he hadn't so far in the fourteen months they had been married...

Perhaps—

Danny...! Obviously Nick didn't believe her about the reason for Danny's telephone call, thought she was going to meet Danny some time during the next few days—and by inviting her out to lunch with him today Nick was making sure she wasn't free to meet Danny!

'I don't have a previous appointment,' she answered him stiffly. 'But I am rather busy. And then there's Jessica to consider—'

'One excuse will suffice as a no, Gemini,' Nick cut in harshly, his expression grim now, his eyes glacial.

'We aren't that busy, Gemini,' Hugh put in lightly, seeming unaware of any tension between the married couple. 'The show is months away yet. And you showed me earlier how to feed Jessica; I would love to look after her for a couple of hours,' he added eagerly.

She couldn't help smiling at his barely concealed ulterior motive. 'She'll be spoilt rotten by the end of today,' she complained ruefully. 'But...okay. If that suits you, Nick?' She looked at him from beneath lowered lashes, suddenly feeling shy at the thought of going out to lunch with her husband—even if his motives for the invitation were suspect!

The two of them never went out alone together. Any dinners or parties they attended always involved business, either Nick's or her own. And even though she knew there was a method in Nick's madness—namely, keeping her well away from Danny!—she was still a little flustered. It would be almost like going out on a date. And that was something they had never done, either!

'Fine,' he accepted tersely, obviously still a little piqued at her initial excuses.

Gemini pulled on a pale plum-coloured silk jacket over her body-hugging black top—the jacket matching the loose trousers she wore—running her fingers through her hair before standing up. 'Ready,' she told Nick brightly.

'My kind of woman,' Nick told Hugh dryly.

Gemini only wished that she were. But unfortunately she knew Nick preferred women—one woman in particular!—who were less conventional and more outgoing than she could ever be.

But they were about to go out and have lunch together. Which was definitely a first!

She couldn't help feeling a little unfair to Hugh as she followed Nick towards the door, and turned to face him. 'Are you really sure you can cope?'

'Of course I'm sure,' Hugh answered indignantly. 'I had lots of kid sisters, remember?' he added wistfully.

Hugh hadn't been lucky in attaining his family's understanding about his sexuality. Those three sisters he spoke of were all married, with children of their own; children they didn't allow their uncle Hugh to see...

Gemini smiled at him warmly. 'Have fun!'

'Oh, we will,' Hugh assured her gratefully.

She looked at Nick from beneath lowered lashes once they were in his car and driving towards the centre of town, not exactly encouraged by the harsh set of his features or the icy narrowing of his eyes The silence between them was filled with tension.

Well, he'd been the one to instigate this lunch together;

it was just too bad if he now found he didn't particularly like the idea!

Gemini blinked back the tears that suddenly filled her eyes, turning to look out the side window, seeing nothing, but unwilling to let Nick see how close to tears she actually was.

'Would you prefer French or Italian?'

She literally jumped a little in her seat when Nick suddenly broke the silence between them, turning to look at him, the tears firmly under control now. 'Sorry...?' She frowned across at him.

Nick glanced at her impatiently before turning his attention back to the road. 'Are you in the mood to eat French or Italian food?' he repeated dryly.

She wasn't in the mood to eat at all; in fact she already regretted being more or less bullied by the two men into coming out with him. But, having accepted the invitation... 'Italian would be fine,' she assured him huskily.

Nick was obviously known at the restaurant he took her to, the waiter greeting him by name before showing them to a table near the window.

Gemini looked across the table at Nick with raised brows once they were seated. 'A favourite haunt of yours?' she questioned dryly; there was so much she didn't know about this husband of hers!

He glanced up from the menu he had been looking through. 'It's just around the corner from my office.' He shrugged.

Gemini had already realised that—and she also knew he had rather a pretty young secretary! 'Convenient,' she drawled mockingly.

Nick's gaze sharpened. 'What's that supposed to mean?' he rasped.

She raised dark brows at his aggression. 'Exactly what I said; this restaurant is convenient for you to come and have a meal during your lunch-break.' Although as he was his own boss he could make that lunch-break as long or short as he wished!

Nick gave a deep sigh. 'Gemini—'

'Nick?' she returned coolly.

Although cool was the last thing she felt. This was not going well. And she knew that she was responsible for most of that. But she simply couldn't relax in Nick's company any more. And the more she thought about it, the more she questioned his motives for bringing her out to lunch today!

Maybe making sure she wasn't free to see Danny wasn't the only reason for this uncharacteristic invitation? After all, Nick still hadn't told her what those 'things' were he had wanted to talk to her about on Saturday evening...

'Could we forget about the tension of the weekend for a while,' he suggested quietly, seeming to have half-read her thoughts, 'and just enjoy having lunch together?'

He could have no idea of just how much she wished that were possible, of how she longed to go back to the way things had been between them during the first six months of their marriage! But the truth of the matter was she was too aware of him, too conscious of her own feelings towards him, to feel in the least relaxed in his company any more!

She gave a slight inclination of her head. 'If that's what you want, Nick.'

'It is,' he sighed. 'I thought we at least liked each other, Gemini, but these last few days—!' He shook his head grimly. 'I'm not even sure that's true any more.'

Gemini certainly liked him. Probably more than she should. She admired his self-confidence, his success, his compassionate way of dealing with business. And as far as he looked—!

She shied away from even looking at him now, firmly turning her attention to her own menu, her pulse racing. 'I think you're exaggerating what happened over the weekend, Nick,' she told him in measured tones. 'Nothing has really changed between us.'

'I don't call the fact that I almost made love to you nothing!' he bit out harshly.

Neither did she, and the warm colour once again entered her cheeks. But when Nick had spoken of forgetting what had happened at the weekend for a few hours, she had thought he'd meant Jemima's and Danny's return to their lives…!

She swallowed hard. 'No one got hurt, Nick,' she dismissed abruptly.

'Didn't they? I—' He broke off as the waiter returned to their table to take their order, and the next few minutes were taken up with choosing their food.

A respite for which Gemini was more than grateful! The two of them kissing and touching each other, 'almost' making love, as Nick had put it, was a cherished memory she could take out and relish whenever she was alone. She certainly didn't want to sit here with Nick and dissect what had happened between them, to pull it apart until it had no meaning whatsoever!

She leant forward once the waiter had gone away, putting her hand briefly over Nick's as it rested on the tabletop. And even that momentary touch was enough to send an electric thrill up her arm and through her body!

'Let's just do as you suggested, Nick, and enjoy lunch,' she said huskily. 'Neither of us will be able to work this afternoon if we end up giving each other indigestion!' she added, in an effort to lighten the conversation.

He looked at her for several long seconds, green eyes narrowed, and then he slowly nodded. 'Truce, Gemini?' he drawled self-derisively.

'Truce, Nick,' she agreed gratefully.

He gave an acknowledging nod. 'How's the collection going?'

Gemini was grateful for the abrupt change of subject. Maybe lunch would be okay, after all...

She gave a rueful smile. 'When I can drag Hugh away from the baby, it's going just fine!'

Nick chuckled softly. 'He would have made a wonderful father, he obviously adores kids.'

'Mm,' she acknowledged wistfully. And not just Hugh, either. Nick would have made a wonderful father too...

'Now I've made you sad again,' Nick muttered self-disgustedly. 'I just can't seem to say the right thing to you at the moment!' He shook his head impatiently.

It wasn't just Nick. Her emotions were all over the place just recently, and the least little thing could produce a mood-swing of almost three hundred and sixty degrees! 'Time of the month,' she dismissed untruthfully; the truth was much more embarrassing than discussing her body clock!

Nick seemed to visibly relax at her explanation, sipping at the red wine the waiter had poured for them both. 'I've always been grateful for that very reason that I was born male.' He grimaced.

'But it has its compensations,' Gemini said with a rueful smile. 'We also get to carry and give birth to the babies,' she explained at his questioning look.

And then instantly regretted her candidness. When had she ever given any indication that she considered being pregnant and giving birth a 'compensation'? When had she ever thought such a thing?

The last few days, she inwardly acknowledged. Since looking after Jessica...

Three days ago she had questioned how she was ever going to cope with having a baby in the house, let alone look after her; now she knew she was going to miss Jessica unbearably when Jemima came to collect her.

There was something so—so emotional, she supposed, about being so completely alone with a baby during the night hours, holding her, talking to her, kissing her, with the rest of the world seeming to be asleep. And unnecessary. It was the most wonderful experience, so difficult to describe, and yet Gemini knew she was going to miss those times with Jessica the most.

Nick's mouth twisted derisively. 'I think most women would find the reality of that statement debatable,' he drawled mockingly.

Gemini laughed softly. 'The reality of it probably is,' she acknowledged self-derisively. 'But we can all dream, Nick,' she added laughingly.

'I thought your dreams were all of fabrics and fashions!' he teased.

'They are.' She nodded, sitting back as their first course was delivered to their table. 'Mmm, this is delicious,' she murmured appreciatively after taking the first mouthful of the pasta she had ordered. 'Although I'm probably going to smell of garlic all day!' she added ruefully.

'Never mind, mine has garlic in, too,' Nick dismissed.

Gemini wondered at the relevance of his remark, but didn't comment on it, continuing to eat her food. They seemed to have reached some level of camaraderie between them again; they were at least talking now, without one or both of them becoming defensive—and she certainly didn't want to be the one who broke that truce!

It was a wonderful meal, the food excellent, and the company too, as Nick set out to amuse her with stories of the nightmare business deal he was trying to put in place at the moment.

Gemini had such a good time that it wasn't until they were driving back to the salon a couple of hours later that she realised Nick hadn't told her the reason for his unexpected invitation out to lunch. Because one thing she did know about Nick: he always had a reason for everything he did.

She turned in the passenger seat to look at him. 'Lovely as the meal was, Nick, you still haven't told me why we had lunch together.'

He quirked dark brows. 'Does there have to be a reason?'

She would have so liked to say no—but she knew better. 'I think so, yes,' she answered him slowly.

Nick's mouth tightened. 'Can't fool you for a minute, can I, Gemini?' he bit out tersely.

She had hoped. Oh, yes, she had hoped... But obviously no! 'Not when you do unexpected things like taking me out to lunch, no,' she said dryly.

He sighed. 'I called round to see Danny this morning, Gemini,' he told her evenly.

Danny, again! Damn it—

'Yes?' she prompted scathingly, sitting tensely in her seat now. 'Did you believe *him* when he told you he only telephoned me because he's trying to contact Jemima?' she asked, her eyes glittering deeply blue.

'He didn't tell me that—he didn't tell me anything, Gemini,' he added as she opened her mouth to object. 'For the simple reason he isn't there. He's gone away, Gemini,' Nick added softly. 'And the caretaker of the building where he lives says he has no idea when Danny will be back!'

And just what did that have to do with her? Gemini wanted to demand. But she knew the answer to that all too well...

Nick believed she was going to be upset at learning Danny had gone away again without seeing her; he had taken her out to lunch so that he could tell her and so soften the blow for her.

Ridiculous. It was absolutely ridiculous that her husband

should feel he had reason to do any such thing. And with Danny's departure, she realised, she had even less chance of convincing Nick of her complete indifference to Danny, or his whereabouts.

She gave a dismissive shrug. 'What does any of this have to do with me, Nick?' she prompted hardily, looking at him challengingly. The friendship renewed between them over lunch was evaporating as if it had never been.

Damn him! How could Nick possibly think her stupid enough to fall for Danny's irresponsible brand of charm all over again? The last time had been a brainstorm—to do it all over again would be sheer madness!

Nick drew the car to a halt outside the salon before answering her, turning in his own seat, his arm along the back of hers. 'I wouldn't like to see you get hurt, Gemini,' he told her huskily.

He had no idea how hurt she already was—from loving him so hopelessly! 'Danny couldn't hurt me, Nick—'

'There's more, Gemini,' he cut in firmly, the hand that rested along the back of her car seat absently playing with the darkness of her hair as it lay silkily on her shoulders. He drew in a deep breath. 'I just don't quite know how to tell you...' he muttered grimly.

'Just spit it out, Nick,' she snapped irritably. 'Nothing you can tell me about Danny would shock me any more!'

Nick nodded impatiently. 'He's my younger brother, and for that reason I love him—but I still know that the next time I see him I'm going to take pleasure in hitting him!'

She shook her head. 'That's between you and Danny,' she bit out.

She wanted to be out of here, back in the privacy of her salon, where she could sit and lick her wounds. Because for Nick to still harbour these violent feelings towards Danny he must still care for Jemima...!

Nick sighed. 'Do you ever call Danny at his apartment, Gemini?' He looked at her searchingly.

Her eyes flashed deeply blue. 'I've already told you; I never call him anywhere! You—'

'I only ask because Danny doesn't live alone any more, Gemini,' Nick cut in forcefully, wincing even as he made the announcement. 'He's been sharing the apartment for the last eight months. With a woman,' he added pointedly.

Gemini stared at him. She didn't know what to say. Danny was actually living with some woman and yet he was still trying to contact Jemima...! Nick was going to have to get in line behind her if he wanted to hit Danny; Gemini wanted to be the first!

Jemima might be irresponsible, but she was still Gemini's sister, and from the mere fact of Jessica's existence, Jemima had been through a traumatic time of her own this last year; she certainly didn't need an outrageous womaniser like Danny Drummond coming back into her life. And Gemini intended telling her as much when she came to collect Jessica!

Gemini swallowed hard, her face pale beneath her makeup. 'Did you meet—this woman?' she prompted woodenly.

Nick shook his head. 'She wasn't in, either,' he rasped. 'But the fact that they've been living together for eight months seems to imply some sort of permanence,' he added, giving Gemini another searching look.

She raised scornful brows at this claim. 'Nothing your brother does ever implies "permanence"!' she said disgustedly. 'The man has invented a whole new dictionary of his own—with his own interpretations!'

'That's it, Gemini.' Nick nodded his approval. 'Don't get sad, get mad!'

It was Jemima she wanted to get mad at Danny, not

herself. She just hoped that she saw her sister before Danny did!

'I have to go, Nick,' she told him frowningly. 'Hugh has been left holding the baby long enough,' she added dryly, turning to open the car door. 'Will you be in for dinner this evening?' she added distractedly as she found Nick holding the door open for her as she stepped out onto the pavement.

'Yes,' he confirmed, looking down at her grimly. 'Will you?'

She looked at him in surprise. 'Of course,' she acknowledged questioningly. 'Until Jemima collects Jessica I'm pretty tied in that way,' she added dryly.

'Of course.' Nick nodded abruptly. 'I'll see you both later, then.'

Gemini hurried away, thankfully closing the salon door behind her, aware that Nick hadn't got back into his car yet, that he had been watching her every move.

'Good lunch?' Hugh enquired lightly as Gemini sank weakly against the closed door.

The food had been excellent, and during the meal the conversation had been too; it was only the last few minutes that had really put a jarring note on the whole thing...

'Fine,' she dismissed, moving to hang up her jacket. 'How's Jessica?'

'Fed. And fast asleep,' Hugh informed her happily, looking over at the carrycot where the baby slept.

'Good.' She sighed her relief.

'Nick seemed a little—grim today?' Hugh added probingly as he turned back to Gemini.

'Nick is always grim,' she bit out tersely, at once regretting her irritability as Hugh raised questioning brows at her. 'Don't ask, Hugh,' she sighed, holding up a protesting hand. 'It's all far too complicated to explain!' She shook her head, feeling those ridiculous tears threatening once again.

In fact, they didn't just threaten, they began to fall hotly down her cheeks!

'Gem!' Hugh sounded totally distressed himself as he pulled her into the warmth of his arms, holding her tenderly against his chest as he patted her back awkwardly.

Gemini cried as she couldn't remember crying for years, deep, racking sobs that shook her whole body, the heated tears seeming to burn her cheeks as they fell unchecked.

She was crying for need of Nick. For want of Nick. For love of Nick. She was just crying for Nick! She loved him so much it was tearing her apart.

And she simply didn't know what to do about it. She loved Nick, and he still appeared to be in love with her sister. And Nick believed she was still somehow involved with Danny. The whole situation was spiralling out of—

'Am I interrupting something?' Nick's voice rasped coldly into the maelstrom of emotions she seemed to have fallen into.

Gemini looked up in shocked surprise from where she stood tenderly cradled in Hugh's bear-hug of affection, gasping softly at the harsh violence in Nick's face as he looked across the room at her from the open doorway where he stood.

'Your bag.' He held it up to explain his unexpected return, his expression so coldly remote as it slowly moved over her from head to toe that Gemini felt a shiver run down her spine. 'You left it in the car. I thought you might need it,' he added contemptuously. 'Hugh.' He nodded dismissively to the other man before turning on his heel and leaving as suddenly as he had appeared, the door slamming behind him.

Hugh looked across at the violently closed door. 'Now what the hell—? Gemini.' He looked down at her frowningly. 'What on earth is going on between you and Nick?'

She began to laugh, a laugh completely without humour,

a laugh that mingled with the tears that had once again begun to fall.

What was going on between Nick and herself?

She wished she knew!

What had ever 'gone on' between them? They had married for the wrong reasons, were still married for the wrong reasons. And if the look on Nick's face just now was anything to go by that marriage wasn't going to last much longer!

CHAPTER SEVEN

GEMINI entered the dining-room quietly, very tall and slender in a short black sheath dress, barely glancing at Nick as she took her seat opposite him at the table.

She hadn't seen Nick since she'd returned to the house from the salon just over an hour ago, her time since taken up with seeing to the baby before settling her down for the evening, and then showering herself before dressing for dinner.

But the last time she'd seen Nick he'd looked at her with such icy contempt that it had taken all of her self-confidence to come downstairs this evening and face him at all!

She drew in a ragged breath, her head tilted defiantly as she forced herself to look at him. 'Before we start our meal perhaps I should explain about earlier—'

'Hugh already did that,' Nick cut in dryly, his mouth twisting mockingly as Gemini gave him a startled look. 'He came to see me at my office,' he explained stiltedly.

Her eyes widened. 'Hugh did?' Hugh had left her at the salon shortly after five o'clock, but he had said nothing about going to see Nick...

Nick gave an inclination of his head. 'He seemed to think that I may have misconstrued the situation between the two of you that I walked in on.'

'Hugh did?' Gemini gasped.

'You're repeating yourself, Gemini,' Nick drawled derisively. 'But if it's any consolation,' he added ruefully, 'I was as surprised as you obviously are that he felt the need

99

to tell me your being in his arms was all perfectly innocent!'

'Well, of course it was perfectly innocent,' she snapped irritably. 'We both know that Hugh is happy in his relationship with Alan. And as for me—' She broke off, glancing across at him awkwardly.

As for her…?

'You're happy in your relationship with me,' Nick finished coldly. 'Except that you aren't,' he added harshly.

'I—' Gemini broke off her protest as Mrs James came in with their smoked salmon starter, smiling her thanks to the older woman as she placed the food in front of them.

Not that Gemini particularly felt like eating. She had known this evening was going to be awkward, but another open confrontation with Nick was something she didn't think she could cope with at the moment.

'Eat your food, Gemini,' Nick instructed abruptly once they were alone again. 'I'm not in the mood for another argument,' he added wearily, picking up his own knife and fork.

Gemini did likewise. 'I have no intention of arguing with you, Nick,' she assured him coolly. 'It's been a long day. I intend eating my dinner before going straight to bed.'

Well…to her bedroom, at least. She needed the peace of her own space. Although after Saturday night even her bedroom wasn't immune to Nick's presence…

Nick's mouth twisted mockingly. 'Ignoring me isn't going to make me go away, Gemini!'

'It would be impossible to ignore you, Nick,' she snapped, her eyes flashing deeply blue. 'The truth of the matter is, working full-time and looking after a baby too is very tiring.' Which was true. It just wasn't the real reason she was going to her bedroom straight after they had eaten…

His expression darkened. 'Jemima is the most selfish—!'

He broke off, shaking his head disgustedly. 'Would you like me to get up to Jessica tonight, to give you a break?'

It was very disconcerting the way he changed from anger to concern in a matter of seconds! If it *was* concern. A bad-tempered wife through lack of sleep was not part of their bargain!

Except her mercurial moods had nothing to do with caring for Jessica...

'I can manage—thank you,' she refused stiltedly.

'Gemini, I was only— Oh, damn it to hell!' Nick threw his knife and fork down onto his plate before standing up. 'I've had enough of this. I'm going to my study!'

Gemini watched him go before putting down her own knife and fork, burying her face in her hands.

How much longer could they go on like this?

Quite what had woken her Gemini wasn't sure. No sound was coming from Jessica's room when she hurried down the hallway to check. Which wasn't surprising; it was only an hour or so ago that she had fed the baby and put her back to bed.

But something had disturbed her sleep, a noise that wasn't usual in the house at two o'clock in the morning. What—?

'I've already told you this behaviour is not acceptable, Jemima.' Nick could be heard almost shouting downstairs in the hallway. 'You simply took off, without a word to anyone, and— Yes, I'm aware you have your work; you've told me that often enough in the past!' he rasped, after what seemed to be an answer to his accusation.

But Gemini hadn't actually heard Jemima speak, which must mean Nick was on the telephone to her!

Gemini stood at the top of the stairs, frozen to the spot, knowing now that it had to have been Nick's raised voice that had woken her so suddenly, but she was unsure about whether or not to make her presence known to him.

Had Jemima telephoned here? Or had Nick been the one to telephone Jemima? Because if it had been the latter then Nick must have known where Jemima was all the time. Which posed a whole lot of other questions.

'The day after tomorrow isn't good enough, Jemima,' Nick rasped now, in answer to something Jemima had said to him. 'I want you back here tomorrow. Yes—tomorrow, Jemima,' he insisted firmly. 'It wasn't fair of you to just dump Jessica on Gemini the way that you did. She— Just a moment. I thought I heard something,' he muttered impatiently.

The 'something' had been Gemini accidentally touching against the vase that stood on a table at the top of the stairs, then reaching out quickly to steady it so that it didn't fall. But obviously not before Nick had heard the faint noise it had made as it wobbled precariously…!

Gemini moved back into the shadows of the gallery as she sensed Nick looking up the stairs into the darkness, the decision about whether or not to show herself made for her in those few seconds. Nick would think it very odd now if she were to suddenly appear at the top of the stairs!

'It was nothing,' Nick dismissed as he returned to the telephone a few seconds later, sounding somewhat calmer now. 'Jemima, I've heard all your excuses before, dozens of times—remember?' he said wearily. 'It's too late for explanations,' he added hardily. 'Just get yourself back here, where you belong!' He slammed the telephone receiver back onto its cradle.

Gemini moved quickly, her bare feet soundless in the carpeted hallway, reaching the sanctuary of her bedroom seconds later and closing the door behind her to lean back against it, her heart beating erratically against the silky material of her blue pyjama top.

There had been nothing in Nick's side of the telephone conversation to tell her who had been the one to initiate the call, and yet... Nick hadn't sounded as if he were talking to a woman he hadn't seen or spoken to for over a year!

Gemini felt sick. Nick and Jemima...? She couldn't bear it.

Gemini sprang away from the door behind her as if it burnt her as a soft knock sounded from the other side.

Nick!

There was no one else it could be. But if he was knocking on her bedroom door at this time of night then he had to know she had been upstairs in the gallery listening, after all...

'Gemini, I know you're awake,' he told her softly, instantly confirming that question.

She might be awake, but that didn't mean she wanted to talk to him! Because she was afraid that if she spoke to Nick at this moment she might just say something she would later regret. That both of them would regret!

'Gem, please open the door...'

She wrenched the door open, glaring at Nick as he stood outside in the hallway wearing only his black silk robe. 'Don't call me that!' she snapped furiously. How dared he? When he had just been speaking to her sister!

He held his hands up defensively. 'Sorry,' he sighed heavily. 'That was Jemima on the telephone—'

'I'm aware of who it was,' she bit out, two angry spots of colour on her cheeks.

Nick looked at her consideringly. 'Then why didn't you come down and speak to her yourself?' Instead of skulking in the shadows at the top of the stairs, his tone seemed to imply!

She hadn't been skulking exactly, only shocked into immobility.

'From what I heard, you were saying all that needed to be said.' More than needed to be said, she would have thought!

His eyes narrowed to green slits. 'And what is that supposed to mean?' His voice was dangerously soft.

Gemini shrugged. 'You told Jemima to come back home.' 'Where she belonged', Gemini inwardly recalled painfully. Did that mean Jemima 'belonged' with Nick...?

Because if it did, that put a completely different light on the whole of Nick's conversation with her sister!

'Of course I did.' He nodded tersely. 'Your sister seems to believe that no one else has work to do, that the whole world revolves around what she wants. I don't— Hell, I don't want to talk about Jemima!' Nick muttered disgustedly, shaking his head. 'I'm sick of talking about her. We seem to have talked about little else the last few days.'

Gemini looked at him with apprehensive eyes. 'Then what do you want to talk about, Nick?'

He gave a humourless smile. 'At two-thirty in the morning? I would rather not be talking at all.' He sighed his impatience with the situation.

Then what would he rather be doing? Gemini wondered with a frown, at once pushing that thought to the back of her mind. If it involved Jemima, then she wouldn't believe him...!

Her marriage seemed to have turned into a no-win situation!

'I'm wide awake now,' Nick bit out tersely. 'Feel like joining me for a cup of cocoa?' he invited.

She wasn't sure what she wanted any more. She knew that she loved Nick, but if he were involved with her sister again...! Much as it might grieve her to do it, if that turned out to be the case she knew she would have to be the one to end their marriage...

'It's only a cup of cocoa, Gemini,' Nick drawled mockingly, 'not a life-threatening decision!'

That depended on what they talked about while they drank their cocoa! But, Gemini realised, burying her head in the sand was not going to change anything.

'Fine,' she accepted abruptly, turning to get her robe, pulling it on over her pyjamas before following Nick out of the room and down the stairs. The ticking of the grandfather clock in the hallway sounded very loud to her ears.

Nick didn't put on the main kitchen lights as they entered the room, moving to click on the light over the Aga, casting a warm glow over the oak kitchen cupboards.

It was that strange time of night again, Gemini realised with dismay, when nothing seemed quite real. Least of all Nick and herself!

'Would you like me to make it?' she asked huskily.

'Certainly not,' he refused firmly. 'I'm more than capable of making my own wife a cup of cocoa.'

His wife... Yes, that was what she was. But in name only...

Once again she wondered if things would be different between them if that were no longer the case. There seemed only one way to find that out!

But could she do it? she wondered as she sipped at the mug of cocoa Nick had made and placed in front of her. Could she actually change this situation by having Nick make love to her? Did she want to?

The answer to that was all too easy to find; until she heard from Nick's own lips that it was Jemima he still cared for, Gemini knew she would do anything to try and salvage their marriage. Anything at all...

'Hey, I didn't mean it literally earlier, about not talking.' Nick teasingly interrupted her thoughts, sitting opposite her at the kitchen table now.

God, he was so good-looking, Gemini groaned inwardly.

The darkness of his hair was ruffled, the hard planes of his face softened by the muted lighting in the room, and the warmth of his body seemed to reach out and enfold her.

'Gemini...?' he questioned uncertainly, his gaze narrowed on her flushed face.

Flushed because she wanted Nick, wanted him so much she physically ached with it. And the way things stood between them now, she knew she had little to lose!

So what if she did make a fool of herself? She was twenty-nine years old, for goodness' sake, not some gauche teenager. Even if she would never get over loving Nick, she *would* recover if he physically rejected her. And there was no reason why Nick should reject her; he'd found her attractive enough the other night. Besides, she was Nick's wife, damn it, and if any woman was entitled to share his bed it was her!

She would not give Nick up without a fight!

'Nick,' she returned huskily, putting down her empty mug as she held his gaze.

Which wasn't so easy to do with Nick looking at her so searchingly. But she forced herself not to let her gaze waver from his, at the same time doing nothing to hide the desire she felt for him.

Nick stood up slowly, coming round the table to pull her to her feet; Gemini stood several inches shorter than him without the benefit of shoes. Nick's hand gently touched beneath her chin as he tilted her face up to his, continuing that searching gaze over her flushed face and feverish eyes.

'Gemini, are you sure this is what you want?' he finally murmured huskily, frowning. 'I realise today has been a difficult time for you—

'Nick, why don't you stop talking and just kiss me?' she groaned, pushing all thoughts of the disastrous day firmly behind her. She was the one here with Nick now, and it would be her that he made love to. She would make sure of that!

'Are you going to regret this tomorrow?' Still Nick hesitated.

'Has no one ever told you, Nick? Tomorrow never comes!' Gemini dismissed unflinchingly.

'That won't stop you hating me,' he sighed.

She put her arms about him, pressing her body warmly against his. 'I like and respect you too much, Nick, to ever hate you,' she assured him huskily.

And it was true. No matter what happened, she wouldn't hate Nick. He had been completely honest with her from the beginning of their marriage, had never made any pretence of loving her, of marrying her for any other reason than that her sister and his brother had both let them down so badly; she was the one who had changed, not Nick.

'Famous last words, Gemini?' he said ruefully, but his arms moved about her waist, pulling her closer against him.

'I don't care—as long as they're the last ones for some time!' she returned dismissively, her face raised invitingly as his mouth at last lowered to hers.

It was as if the hours since Saturday night, since she had last been in Nicks arms, had never happened; that fiery passion was instantly rekindled, setting Gemini on fire, her body curving into the warm hardness of his.

He felt so good, his shoulders broad and muscled beneath her fingertips, his chest lightly covered with dark hair as she pushed aside his robe, the nakedness of his thighs strong and powerful.

'Gemini—'

'No talking,' she reminded him, placing her fingers lightly over his lips.

He smiled down at her, gently kissing each fingertip before removing her hand, but keeping it held tightly in his. 'I was only going to suggest we go upstairs to bed—unless you want me to make love to you on the kitchen table?' he teased huskily.

She laughed softly. 'Novel—but I doubt it would be very comfortable!'

Her hand remained clasped in his as they went slowly up the stairs together. Gemini was feeling slightly shy now, but determined, nevertheless, to see this through. Anything to make it harder for Nick to end their marriage!

By tacit agreement it was her bedroom they went to, the bedside lamp still on from when Gemini had switched it on earlier, after being woken by Nick's raised voice down in the hallway.

'Leave it,' Nick encouraged softly as she would have reached out and switched off the lamp. 'Unless you mind—?' Being swept away on a tide of passion as they had been on Saturday night, and again a few minutes ago downstairs, was one thing, but— 'No,' she assured him huskily. 'I don't mind.'

Nick drew in a ragged breath, reaching out to untie her robe and slip it off her shoulders before letting it fall onto the carpeted floor at their feet, the blue silk top quickly following it.

'You're beautiful, Gemini,' he murmured throatily, gently cupping each of her breasts before bending his head and kissing each fiery tip.

She groaned low in her throat, her legs feeling suddenly weak. Her back arched as Nick's tongue moistly caressed each breast, seeming to savour the taste of her, and trembling pleasure coursed through the whole of her body.

Nick's lips blazed a trail of fire down her ribcage to her navel, his tongue caressing the tiny cavern before his lips moved even lower. Gemini's blue silk trousers fell fluidly to the floor as he released the single button from its fastening, leaving her completely naked before him.

Gemini gasped, her fingers becoming entangled in the

dark thickness of his hair, her body arching in aching need as those caressing lips moved across her thighs.

Nick's eyes were dark with passion as he looked up at her. 'If you want me to stop—'

'I don't,' she assured him breathlessly. 'Please!'

'God, Gemini..!' His arms were about her thighs as he briefly held her to him before standing up. 'Now me,' he invited huskily, standing back slightly so that she could reach the belt to his robe.

But even so Gemini's fingers fumbled with the single fastening. She was trembling with desire, and yet at the same time wanting to savour Nick's body as he had just drunk in all of her.

Totally naked, there was only one word to describe Nick, the same word he had used to describe her minutes ago: beautiful.

It seemed a strange word to associate with the hard, arrogant man who was her husband, but it was still the only word Gemini could think of to describe the lithe planes of his body, the dark hair on his chest, moving in a vee down to his muscular thighs, his legs, long and powerful. There was not an ounce of superfluous flesh on the whole of his body.

Gemini moved, kissing his chest as he had kissed her, rewarded by his sharply indrawn breath as he tried to stay motionless before her. Tried, because as her lips ad hands followed the same path over his body as his had over hers Nick was finding it more and more difficult to withstand those kisses and caresses.

'No more, Gemini!' he groaned. 'Not unless you want me to totally lose control!' He reached down and pulled her effortlessly to her feet, his face contorted almost painfully at the effort it had taken to stop those caressing hands and lips.

He threw back the bedclothes before gently laying her

down, quickly joining her, his mouth once more claiming hers.

It was like drowning, being washed away on a tide of weightlessness, no thought possible, only feeling. Feeling such as Gemini had never known before. Nick taking her again and again to the brink of total mindlessness.

No part of her remained untouched or unkissed by him; every curve and hollow, explored and captured, became his for the taking.

And Nick's body became as familiar to her as her own, every muscle, every smooth contour lovingly touched as she kissed him in return.

She was so roused now that the low sounds in her throat had turned from ones of pleasure to pleading; she wanted him inside her, to know his full possession.

'Not yet,' he groaned, his head against her breasts. 'I never want this to end!'

She didn't want it to end, either, wanted it to be their beginning...!

'Please, Nick,' she sighed achingly, her legs moistly entwined with his, reaching down to cup his face with her hands, looking down intently into his passion-flushed face. 'Say it, Nick,' she encouraged longingly. 'Say my name!' Her voice broke emotionally.

'Gemini...?' he repeated dazedly. 'Gemini, Gemini, Gemini!' He groaned shakily.

She gave a breathless laugh. 'Make love to me, Nick. Please!'

With one last slightly puzzled look he shifted slightly, and they were finally one...

So closely entwined were they now that Gemini wasn't sure where she ended and Nick began, and as he began to move slowly inside her she didn't particularly care!

He had filled her with burning pleasure before, but now she was consumed, totally lost, falling over that precipice time and time again before she felt Nick totally lose control himself, his body arching slightly before he surrendered to his own pleasure, taking her with him to a plateau of sensation she hadn't known existed.

Only the sound of their ragged breathing filled the air now, and Nick reached down to pull the bedclothes up over their rapidly cooling bodies, resting her head on his shoulder as his arms gathered her close against him.

Gemini knew she should say something, anything, but as deep, satisfied tiredness washed over her she knew it would have to wait, that she couldn't have spoken now even if she'd tried.

But she was with the man she loved, held protectively against the warmth of his body. And he was going to stay exactly where he was, had no intention of returning to his own bedroom after their lovemaking, as she had once dreaded he might. For the moment it was enough…

Gemini had no idea what time it was when she woke the next morning, but she could see the sun shining brightly behind her bedroom curtains so it had to be somewhere around breakfast time. Not that she had any appetite. Not for food, anyway…!

She smiled to herself, remembering all that had happened the night before, that smile fading as she turned over and discovered she was alone in her big double bed, that there was no Nick lying beside her.

But he had been there—hadn't he…? It hadn't all been a dream, as it had so many other nights—had it?

No, it hadn't been a dream, she realised as she moved, her body aching from the unaccustomed lovemaking, a pleasurable ache. She remembered that Nick had woken her again some time during the night. Their second lovemaking, now that they were familiar with each other, had been even more enjoyable than their first.

But where was Nick now?

She sat up on the side of the bed, her cheeks feeling hot as she looked down at her own nakedness, seeing the marks of Nick's passion against her creamy breasts, the slight redness that indicated he had been in need of a shave.

But she was glad of those marks, knew they were confirmation that everything about last night was real, and not a dream after all.

She was humming softly to herself as, once again dressed in the blue silk pyjamas, she sat in front of the mirror to brush the tangles from her dark hair. A smile once again curved her lips as she remembered the way Nick had buried his face and hands in that silky darkness, and that smile remained on her face as a knock sounded on the bedroom door.

She turned on the bedroom stool. 'Come in,' she invited huskily.

'Breakfast, Mrs Drummond.' Mrs James bustled into the room with a laden tray. 'Mr Drummond thought you might like breakfast in bed after your disturbed night,' she explained as she turned to put the tray down on the bedside table.

Disturbed night...! How apt. And this time it had been 'disturbed' for exactly the reason Hugh had supposed yesterday!

But Gemini was glad of the housekeeper's preoccupation with the tray at that moment, giving her a few minutes to cover up her disappointment that it hadn't been Nick at the door. Although he no longer had any reason to bother knocking...

'That was kind of him,' she murmured a little shyly. 'Where is Nick this morning?' she enquired casually as she stood up to pour herself a cup of coffee.

The housekeeper looked surprised at the question. 'Gone to his office, as usual, I presume,' she dismissed.

'Oh.' Gemini had to bite back her feelings of disappointment. Part of her had hoped that Nick might take today off to be with her... Silly, really. Just because her whole world felt different, that didn't mean that Nick's felt the same way! It could just mean that he felt as shy about last night as she did. Not that he ever gave the impression of being shy about anything, but making love to his wife, not once but twice, was not a normal occurrence!

'He did feed Jessica before he left, so she's quite happy,' the housekeeper informed her lightly. 'I'll bring her up to you in a few minutes, if you'd like? Once you've had time to enjoy your breakfast, of course,' she added ruefully.

'That would be lovely,' Gemini accepted distractedly, still disappointed that Nick had gone to work as usual. It would have been nice to wake up in bed with him this morning, to perhaps make love once again...!

But perhaps she was expecting too much too soon. Nick must feel as disorientated himself this morning as she did, unsure quite where they went next. They were bound to feel a little awkward with each other after last night, so perhaps he was right to put a little distance between them for a few hours, give them both chance to sit back and reflect.

Although Gemini knew if she sat and thought about last night too much she wouldn't want to do anything else today, would instead succumb to sensual lethargy. God, she felt good this morning, happily content, determined that nothing was going to disturb her air of well-being.

And for the next few minutes nothing did. The coffee was hot and strong, as she liked it, and the croissants were warm, tasting delicious with honey on them. She even sang to herself as she took her shower before dressing in a figure-hugging dress that same colour blue as her eyes.

A glance at the bedside clock showed her it was a little after nine o'clock, which meant she really should have been on her way to the salon by now, but as last night had effectively been her wedding night she felt she was entitled to be a little dreamy and preoccupied this morning.

Even Jessica, when Mrs James brought her upstairs half an hour later, seemed attuned to her mood, wide awake and gurgling happily in her baby-carrier. Gemini couldn't resist picking her up and cuddling her, and was rewarded with what looked like an actual smile.

Maybe after last night—

'She really is the loveliest baby, isn't she?' Mrs James lingered in the bedroom, obviously loath to leave her young charge.

'Beautiful,' Gemini agreed unhesitatingly. 'No doubt she'll break a few hearts when she's older!' She laughed softly before burying her face briefly in the baby's wonderfully soft talc-smelling neck.

'No doubt,' the housekeeper agreed indulgently. 'That lovely dark hair and green eyes like a cat are sure to be a lethal combination!' she added ruefully.

'Her eyes are blue,' Gemini corrected absently as she held up an ornament from her dressing-table for the baby to look at.

Mrs James laughed softly. 'All newborn babies' eyes are blue,' she dismissed with a shake of her head. 'But that often changes after a few weeks, and Jessica's eyes are already starting to turn green.'

Green…?

Jessica's eyes were going to be green…?

Gemini looked down at the baby, frowning. The last time she had really looked at Jessica's eyes they'd been a clear sky-blue, but she could see now that there was a darker rim to that lightness, a rim of smudgy emerald-green…

She swallowed hard, placing the baby carefully back in her seat. Gemini knew only one other person with emerald-green eyes…

And that person was Nick!

CHAPTER EIGHT

'Twice in as many days,' Hugh murmured speculatively. 'Anyone would think you were in love, Nick!'

Gemini had been aware of the salon door opening, had also known by the sudden tingling sensation down the length of her spine that the person who had opened that door was Nick.

But she hadn't turned from what she was doing, was continuing to drape lilac silk around the mannequin. Although her hands trembled and her breathing suddenly felt constricted.

Jessica had green eyes!

Gemini had been horrified earlier when Rachel James had pointed that fact out to her, had come to only one conclusion. And that conclusion, following on from the night she had just spent in Nick's arms, was totally unacceptable to her.

Nick was Jessica's father!

It just had to be. Admittedly Jemima had been involved with Danny for a short time, but he had brown eyes...! It was too much of a coincidence that Nick and Gemini had once been engaged to marry each other—that Nick still seemed to be in contact with Jemima—and that Jemima's baby had Nick's green eyes.

No wonder Jemima had felt no qualms about sending her baby here; she probably felt that looking after Jessica for just a few days was the least Nick could do, in the circumstances! Except that it also brought Gemini in contact with the baby...

Gemini had felt sick earlier at that realisation, putting the baby down as quickly as she was able to without drawing Mrs James's attention to the fact that just holding Jessica made Gemini feel ill!

She had had to get out of the house, away from her own memories of what had happened between herself and Nick the previous night. So she'd come to the salon, often her refuge in the past, but today she was hoping that it would be her salvation.

But even that had proved a little awkward when she'd first arrived. Hugh had been worried in case he might only have aggravated the situation last night by going to see Nick at his office, to explain things to him, rather than actually helping Gemini as he had intended doing. It had taken Gemini some time to assure Hugh that his visit to Nick hadn't caused a problem between Nick and herself!

After this morning she wasn't sure anything would be able to make matters worse between herself and Nick!

The last thing she wanted, or needed, was for Nick to follow her here!

What was he doing here? Admittedly, as Hugh had just pointed out, it was about the same time Nick had arrived the day before, intent on taking her out to lunch, but that couldn't be the reason he was here again today—could it?

But why couldn't it? she asked self-derisively. The only thing that had changed for Nick since yesterday was that the two of them had spent the night together; he was totally unaware of the fact that she was now also aware that Jessica must be *his* daughter!

Bastard! Swine! Adulterer!

Gemini wasn't too sure whether the last one had applied to Nick when their own marriage had been a paper one only—but it applied now!

She wanted to scream and shout, to hit something—preferably Nick!

But what she actually did was to calmly put down her

tin of pins before turning, her expression cool as she looked enquiringly across the room at Nick.

Which wasn't easy to do when she could clearly remember the intimacies they had shared the night before! She felt sick inside as she recalled the way she had given herself to Nick so freely, making love to him in the same way. And all the time—!

'What can I do for you, Nick?' she rasped harshly, blue eyes flashing with her resentment.

His own eyes narrowed at her aggression. Green eyes…!

'As you can see, I'm very busy.' She indicated the mannequin she and Hugh had been working on until Nick had interrupted them seconds ago.

Nick's gaze narrowed even more, studying her assessingly, his mouth tightening grimly as he obviously didn't like what he found. 'I didn't expect you to come in to work today,' he murmured distractedly.

What had he expected? That she would wait languorously in bed for his return, when they could continue where they had left off the previous night? The sad fact of the matter was that if her earlier conversation with Mrs James had never taken place that was probably exactly what she would have done!

She cringed now as she remembered her satiated dreaminess this morning, her conviction that she and Nick could really make a success of their marriage. And all the time he was Jessica's father! She was sure of it.

The one thing Gemini wasn't sure of was whether or not Nick himself was actually aware of the fact…

She had come to know Nick this last year, didn't believe him to be the sort of man who would shirk the responsibility of fatherhood—but she hadn't believed him to be the sort of man who had an affair with one woman while married to another, either!

But, aware of being Jessica's father or not, Nick *did*

know he had continued his relationship with Jemima after marrying Gemini—and for that Gemini would never be able to forgive him.

'Why not?' she returned challengingly. 'You did.'

He shrugged, still standing over by the door he had closed behind him. 'I had a couple of things to deal with in the office before I could be free for the day,' he dismissed, still looking at her questioningly. 'I was surprised when I got back to the house and found only Mrs James there taking care of Jessica.'

Gemini had left the baby with Mrs James because she hadn't felt able to deal with Jessica at that moment. There was no doubting that she loved the baby, that out of all of them Jessica was completely innocent in all of this, but Gemini just couldn't look at the baby now without seeing those green eyes...!

'Jessica would only have been in the way today.' She shot Hugh an apologetic grimace as he made a protesting sound at this statement. 'As I've already said.' Gemini turned back to Nick. 'I'm very busy.'

'Too busy to eat lunch?' he invited softly.

In a word—yes! Oh, not because she really was busy—but because there was no way she could eat anything, and certainly not in Nick's company!

'I'm afraid so,' she answered dismissively. 'But don't let us keep you from your meal,' she added contemptuously.

Nick's mouth tightened as he easily picked up on that tone. 'I'm not particularly hungry myself,' he drawled lightly, making no effort to leave.

'Well, I am.' Hugh had obviously had enough of this guarded conversation. 'If you'll excuse me, Gemini.' He shot her a teasing grin as she looked at him sharply. 'I gave Alan a broad hint last night that he hasn't taken me out to lunch for yonks, so he suggested taking me today. I, of course, accepted!' He turned to pick up his jacket. 'Have fun!' he called out as he let himself out of the salon.

Coward, Gemini inwardly fumed. She didn't doubt that Hugh did have a luncheon engagement today, but she'd also been aware of the wide-eyed looks he'd given both Nick and herself as their conversation had ping-ponged sharply across the room; it was a look that had clearly said, I have no idea what's going on, but I definitely feel in the way—and I'm out of here!

His fast exit left behind a tension that was impossible not to be aware of. Nick had moved aside to let the other man leave, but otherwise he kept up his defensive stance in front of the door.

Hours ago, Gemini had been filled with euphoria, sure that last night had been a turning point in her marriage to Nick; he'd made love to her as if he cared about her at least, even if he wasn't in love with her. This morning Gemini had been filled with shy excitement at the thought of seeing him again. Now all she felt was a sickness in the pit of her stomach...!

'I only went in to my office today so I could clear my diary, in the belief the two of us would be spending the day together.' Nick spoke softly, questioningly.

Because he didn't know, couldn't know, her heart was breaking!

She forced a dismissive shrug. 'Wouldn't you have been better consulting me first before you did something like that?'

'Gemini—'

'Nick?' she returned—much as she had done last night. Except there was no husky invitation in her voice this time!

'I don't understand this!' Nick exploded impatiently, moving forcefully into the room. 'What the hell is going on Gemini? Last night—'

'Was very pleasant, Nick,' she cut in smoothly. 'I thought you had enjoyed it as much as I did?'

'Of course I enjoyed it, damn it—'

'Then stop making a federal case out of it,' Gemini interrupted lightly, turning away from the pale grimness of his face, picking up her pin tin once again to pin the lilac silk in place.

Totally haphazardly!

The silk was going to be ruined, and Hugh would probably have one of his not infrequent fits of hysteria, but she had to do something, was no longer able to look at Nick. How could he actually manage to look hurt by her coldness? It just wasn't fair!

The first she knew of Nick having crossed over to where she made a pretence of working was when her arm was grasped in his iron-like grip as he swung her round to face him. Her head went back as she looked up at him, her chin jutting out defiantly as she forced herself to meet his furious gaze.

That clash of gazes went on for what seemed like for ever to Gemini, but she wouldn't allow herself to be the first to look away, forcing herself to continue looking Nick straight in the eyes.

'So it's like that, is it?' He was the one to finally break the icy tension between them, abruptly releasing her before stepping back, a nerve pulsing in his rigidly clenched jaw. 'What happened to ''no regrets'', Gemini?' he challenged accusingly.

She swallowed hard. 'I don't regret last night, Nick,' she assured him coolly.

And the effort to keep up that coolness in the face of his obviously bewildered fury was costing her dearly. What she really wanted to do was launch herself into his arms and forget all about that damning conversation she had had with

Mrs James this morning. Except that she couldn't forget it...

Nick shook his head. 'You certainly don't have the look of a woman who wants to repeat it!' he ground out savagely.

She gave a humourless smile. 'Well, not at this particular moment, no,' she replied mockingly, indicating the mannequin she was working on.

'Not at all, from the way you've behaved since I arrived!' he muttered angrily. 'Hell, Gemini, where do we go from here?' he asked disgustedly.

She knew where she would like to go. She would like to hide herself away somewhere until all of this was over and settled. Because she had a feeling it *was* all over between them; she just didn't have the courage yet to hear either of them actually come out and say so...

She gave him a scathing glance. 'I don't think my place of work is any more the place to discuss this than it is to repeat what happened last night.'

'Is there a suitable place to talk about this?' he cut in forcefully, running a hand through the dark thickness of his hair. 'If you remember, I thought we should have talked last night—'

'Oh, wonderful,' she returned. 'Blame what happened last night on me, Nick, why don't you?' She glared across at him, genuinely furious with him, but at the same time relieved to have somewhere to focus her seesaw emotions.

He shook his head. 'I didn't say that,' he said wearily. 'No one is to blame for last night, God damn it,' he rasped. 'But what happened to liking and respecting me too much to ever hate me?' He harshly reminded her of what she had said to him last night. 'Because, let me tell you, you're giving a damned good impression of hating me at this moment!' he informed her grimly.

Probably because a part of her did. But not because of

last night. That was something that she'd wanted for a very long time, and at no time during last night had Nick made any hollow promises of love. No, no matter what happened, she'd already decided that she wouldn't regret last night...

'I think you're imagining things, Nick,' she dismissed lightly. 'I certainly don't hate you.' Not for last night, anyway...!

He stepped forward. 'Gemini—'

'No, I don't hate you, Nick,' she repeated, terrified in case he actually touched her again. Because her traitorous body had quivered with response seconds ago when he'd clasped her arm. 'But neither do I intend acting like some lovesick teenager simply because we spent the night together,' she added, rewarded by the dangerous narrowing of his eyes. 'We aren't either of us children, Nick, and last night was—enjoyable—'

'It was fantastic, damn it!' Nick cut in gratingly, his hands clenched at his sides.

'Possibly,' she agreed dryly. 'I really wouldn't know— probably because I have less experience to draw on for— comparison!'

Nick was ten years older than her, for one thing, and those ten years had not been spent as a celibate bachelor. Beside, she had spent those same last ten years building up her fashion label, with little time for relationships. Except that brief time with Danny... 'You had Danny,' Nick reminded her, seeming to guess at least some of her thoughts. His expression was contemptuous, his gaze scornful as it swept over the slender curvaceousness of her body.

Gemini raised dark brows. 'You surely aren't asking me for that comparison...?' she challenged softly.

'No, damn it, I'm not!' That nerve was once again pulsing in his rigidly clenched jaw. 'Danny is the last person I came here to talk about—'

'You said you came to invite me out to lunch,' she reminded him tautly, knowing she had pushed him too far, anxious now to just finish this conversation. Before she made a complete idiot of herself in front of Nick and began to cry! 'I've explained I'm too busy today. Couldn't we continue this conversation at home later this evening?' When she might—just might—feel strong enough to deal with it!

Nick shook his head slowly. 'As I see it, we have nothing else to say to each other—'

'I didn't say that,' she interrupted quickly; their marriage might be over, but she needed to come to terms with that herself before it was made final! 'Just not now, Nick, hmm?' she added encouragingly.

'"Not now, Nick",' he parroted furiously. 'You sound like a woman that's been married for twenty years, not one!' he dismissed scathingly. 'Okay, Gemini, we'll do this your way; we'll talk later, in the privacy of our own home.' He strode purposefully over to the door, wrenching it open. 'Just don't expect to like any of what I have to say!'

The salon seemed to reverberate with the slamming of the door behind him, and Gemini's legs were feeling just as shaky as she gratefully lowered herself down into a chair.

What was she going to do?

One thing she *had* discovered in the last ten minutes: she still loved Nick!

And it was all for nothing. Because she couldn't continue being married to him now. Not because of last night. That was a beautiful memory that would probably haunt her for the rest of her life.

But there was no way to get past the fact of Jessica...

'What's going on, Gemini?' Hugh frowned down at her, having returned from lunch to find her still collapsed in the chair she had sunk down onto after Nick's furious depar-

ture. 'And don't tell me nothing,' he added firmly as
Gemini would have spoken. 'I've known you too long, and
Nick for over a year, to be foisted off with that answer!'

She gave him a wan smile. 'Why should you think that
anything is going on, Hugh?' she attempted to dismiss.

'I don't think it; I know it!' He sat down next to her.
'The two of you have been different this week—'

'You mean Nick has,' Gemini taunted dryly.

Hugh shook his head. 'I mean you both have. Look, you
know I care for you, Gemini.' He took one of her hands in
his much larger ones. 'And I want more than anything for
you to be happy—and don't say you are.' He halted her
speech once again, giving her a reproving look. 'If this is
happy, then I was happy for years and just didn't realise
it!' he added self-derisively.

Gemini squeezed one of his hands. 'Could we just leave
it, Hugh? For now,' she added pleadingly as he looked
about to protest. 'I will talk to you about it, I promise.' It
would be impossible not to, once she and Nick parted. 'Just
not now,' she added chokingly.

'You see.' Hugh pounced frowningly. 'Even this isn't
like you.' He indicated the tears in her eyes. 'I've never
seen you cry before, and now you've done it twice in as
many days.' He shook his head. 'You've always been so
together, Gemini, so certain of where you were going—'

'I think I've taken a wrong turning,' she cut in emotionally, attempting a smile that didn't quite come off.

'Not in your marriage to Nick?' Hugh's frown deepened.
'Because if that's what you think, Gemini, you're wrong.
Nick's the best thing that ever happened to you,' he said
with certainty. 'Or does all of this have something to do
with Danny Drummond?' he added grimly.

'Danny?' She gaze a puzzled frown. Why on earth
should Hugh think—?

'He telephone here yesterday, Gemini,' Hugh told her evenly.

'Danny did?' Her frown deepened.

Hugh nodded. 'While you were out to lunch with Nick. I have to admit, with looking after Jessica and the state you were in when you came back, I initially forgot to mention the call to you, but even when I did eventually remember I deliberately chose not to tell you,' he admitted grimly. 'I'm sorry, Gemini,' he sighed as she looked across at him with wide eyes. 'But you know I never liked the man.'

No, Hugh had never liked Danny. And the dislike had been mutual. Danny hadn't been able to get past the fact of Hugh's sexuality, and it had shown in his behaviour towards the other man. Hugh, being the sensitive soul that he was, in spite of looking like a boxer or a rugby player, had been well aware of Danny's attitude.

Not that that was enough reason for Hugh to return the dislike; Hugh just hadn't liked anything about Danny, either—not his lifestyle, his complete disregard for other people's feelings, or the way he'd breezed in and out of Gemini's life whenever he felt like it.

But still, Gemini was surprised at Hugh's tardiness in telling her of Danny's call...

'Did he say why he was calling?' She made her voice deliberately casual.

Hugh grimaced. 'Something about going out of town for a few days,' he recalled derisively. 'As if that's of any interest to you— It isn't, is it, Gemini?' He looked at her searchingly as the thought suddenly occurred to him. 'Gem, no!' In his agitation he completely forgot her dislike of that shortened version of her name. 'You're married to Nick now—'

'I'm not sure how much longer that will last,' she admitted heavily.

'What!' Hugh looked horrified. 'But the two of you love each other. You—'

'I love Nick,' she corrected wearily, too tired to even attempt to hide her own feelings. 'I'm not sure what Nick feels for me, but it certainly isn't love.'

'Rubbish!' Hugh dismissed impatiently. 'Of course he loves you. He's always loved you. How could he not love someone as wonderful as you...?' he added dazedly as she looked unimpressed by the claim.

'I think you could be slightly biased, Hugh,' she chided, patting his arm affectionately. 'But thank you, anyway.' At this moment she needed to know someone loved her!

Hugh still frowned. 'You aren't involved with Danny Drummond again, are you, Gemini?'

'Now you've gone and ruined your earlier compliment.' She laughed softly, shaking her head. 'Believe me, my opinion of Danny is no higher than yours!'

'Then why—? Damn it, Gemini, this is none of my business—I know it isn't—and I'm the last person to tell anyone how they should live their life! It's just that—Nick is worth a hundred Dannys!' he added grimly.

A thousand, to Gemini's way of thinking. At least he had been until this morning, when she had looked into Jessica's green eyes...

She drew in a ragged breath. 'Nick isn't everything he appears to be,' she said enigmatically. 'Now, would you mind, Hugh, if I went home for the day? I—I have a headache.' She grimaced. It wasn't a headache exactly, more like a lead weight siting on top of her head. And in her heart! And she very much doubted that she would find Nick at home—despite having 'cleared his diary' for the day! He hadn't given the impression when he'd left here earlier that he was in the mood for the comforts—or otherwise!—of their mutual home!

'You're the boss,' Hugh accepted lightly, turning towards the mannequin they had been working on earlier. 'I think I'll just carry on with— My God, Gemini, what the hell—?'

Her laughter cut off his horrified—and totally predictable!—reaction to the state of the lilac silk after her earlier efforts. 'Just scrap it and start again,' she advised as she picked up her bag prior to leaving.

'I think it's probably as well you've decided to call it a day…!' Hugh was still looking aghast at the ruined silk as Gemini let herself out.

She had, Gemini realised heavily, decided to 'call it a day' in several areas of her life. When she had believed she might stand a chance of fighting for Nick she had had some hope, but it looked as if Jessica's parentage finished all that. And the realisation of that made her feel physically sick.

Part of her still so much wanted not to have to say goodbye to Nick. But another part of her, the part that acknowledged too much had happened for them to continue, knew she couldn't carry on now that she was so tangibly aware of Nick's continued relationship with Jemima.

By the time Gemini reached home her headache was very real, the pain behind her eyes making her feel ill. All she wanted to do was go straight to bed and fall asleep. Hopefully, at the same time, she could forget the last five hours had ever happened!

There seemed little hope of doing that when she arrived home, to find Jemima comfortably ensconced in the kitchen, a gurgling Jessica curled up in her arms, drinking coffee with Mrs James!

CHAPTER NINE

'GEMINI!' Jemima greeted her warmly, standing up to hug the numbed Gemini, who stood in the kitchen doorway. 'We weren't expecting you home just yet— Hey, are you okay, sis?' She looked searchingly at Gemini. 'You look a little green around the gills!'

Green...!

Gemini didn't even want to think about that particular colour! And, no, she wasn't okay; she hadn't seen her twin for over a year, in the last few hours it had become apparent that her own marriage to the man she loved was going to end, and yet as she looked at Jemima all she could think was that it felt good to see her sister once again...!

Illogical. Totally illogical. But it had always been this way between Jemima and herself, their bondship as identical twins so much deeper than that of ordinary siblings. And, strangely, their year of estrangement hadn't changed that...

'No, I'm not okay, as it happens,' Gemini answered faintly, putting up a hand to her thumping temple. 'I came home early because I have a migraine.'

'That's new, isn't it?' Jemima stood back consideringly, every inch her normal buoyant, boisterous self. Pregnancy and motherhood hadn't added any extra weight to the leanness of her frame, although the darkness of her hair was a little longer, adding a softness to the usual angles of her face.

Yes, it was new—but then so were a lot of things in her life recently! 'When did you get back?' Gemini put her bag

down, moving further into the kitchen—and away from
Jemima and the beautiful but painful reminder of Jessica!

'I—'

'I picked her up from the airport a couple of hours ago,'
Nick announced abruptly as he strode forcefully into the
room. He'd changed out of the suit he had been wearing
earlier, and was now wearing a dark green shirt with black
trousers.

Gemini's breath caught in her throat and she felt herself
go even paler as she looked at her husband, in every sense
of the word, once again shaken by the very maleness of
him. But until this moment she hadn't realised Nick was in
the house too...

And he had collected Jemima from the airport...? In all
the times Gemini had been away on business he'd never
done as much for her!

'Wasn't it kind of him?' Jemima said appreciatively,
smiling warmly at Nick.

He shot her an irritated glance. 'Kindness had nothing to
do with it,' he snapped. 'Jessica is your daughter; you
should be the one looking after her.'

Jemima looked unabashed. 'At this stage in her life
Jessica doesn't have a clue who is looking after her, just
as long as someone feeds her,' she dismissed. 'And in the
circumstances—'

'Damn the circumstances,' Nick bit out gratingly, looking sharply across at Gemini, his gaze narrowing as he took
in her paleness. 'I called the salon just now, to let you know
Jemima was here, and Hugh said you had already left because you aren't feeling well.' His dark gaze was probing
now.

'Mrs Drummond has a migraine,' Mrs James put in helpfully, giving Gemini an encouraging smile.

Well, at least someone was on her side! And Gemini
badly needed for someone to be at this moment. Nick might

have tried to telephone her to let her know Jemima was here, but Jemima had just openly mentioned those 'circumstances' that had made her feel she had the right to leave Jessica here in the first place...!

Nick strode impatiently across the room to lift Gemini's chin and look down at her with searching intensity. 'You should be in bed,' he finally told her huskily.

It was where she most wanted to be, with the covers firmly pulled over her head, until Jemima, and the trouble she always brought with her, went away!

At the same time Gemini knew that hiding herself away in her bedroom wouldn't change anything, that the three of them were in a triangle, and only she, it seemed, was uncomfortable in its confines. But with Mrs James present, Gemini didn't see how she could say all that!

She moved pointedly away from Nick's restraining hand, ignoring the anger that flared briefly in his eyes as she did so. *He* was angry? He hadn't seen anything yet!

'That's exactly where I intend going,' she told them all dismissively, picking up her bag once again, deliberately not looking directly at any of them. 'I take it you'll be gone when I come down later?' she added sharply to Jemima as she reached the door; her sister had better be gone—long gone!

Jemima glanced at Nick. 'Nick has offered to drive me home,' she acknowledged huskily.

'With all of Jessica's things, and your own luggage too, it's impractical for you to do anything else,' he bit out impatiently.

Nick was driving Jemima home... Well, what else had she expected? The two of them probably had a lot to talk about. Obviously, with Jemima now having openly talked of those 'circumstances' concerning her leaving Jessica here in the first place, if Nick hadn't known of the baby's parentage before he certainly did now!

She gave Jemima a scathing glance. 'I suppose we should just be grateful that someone is still able to talk some sense into you.' She gave an impatient sigh as Jemima just looked puzzled by the statement. 'Nick told you to come home, and, lo and behold, here you are!' she scorned.

'I wish I could take the credit for that,' Nick said dryly, his mouth twisting as he looked irritably across at Jemima. 'Apparently her story broke last night, and she had to come home anyway,' he explained to Gemini disgustedly.

She should have known! Motherhood hadn't changed Jemima at all. And it was Jessica that Gemini was concerned about. She had become very fond of the baby these last few days, more than fond, and the thought of her going back to Jemima's haphazard idea of parenthood did not fill her with confidence for Jessica's well-being.

Although the baby looked contented enough in her mother's arms. Having been fed and changed, Jessica had now fallen asleep. The sleep of the innocent...

Gemini's mouth tightened angrily. 'Then Nick had better drive you home, hadn't he?' she told her sister with sharp dismissal. 'No need to hurry back, either, Nick,' she added hardily. 'I shall be asleep when you come home.'

His mouth thinned into a narrow line at her obvious message: not only would she be asleep, but she didn't want to be disturbed, either. For any reason!

'I'll come up with you and see you settled before I leave,' he said calmly, quiet challenge in his face as she turned to look at him.

'I think I can manage, Nick; I've been putting myself to bed since I was eight years old!' Gemini scorned harshly.

She didn't want him to come upstairs to her bedroom with her; she had nothing to say to him. Not at this moment, anyway. No doubt there would be plenty for them both to say later...

'Don't be silly, Gemini.' Jemima was the one to rebuke her teasingly. 'You obviously aren't well, and I'm in no hurry to leave. And, from the look of her—' she glanced down affectionately at the baby asleep in her arms '—neither is Jessica!'

She was sure her sister *wasn't* in a hurry to leave; Jemima probably wished now she hadn't been so stupid fifteen months ago, that this was her own home instead of Gemini's—and that Nick was hers too! Well, perhaps in time he still would be...

'It's because Gemini has been caring for Jessica that she has ended up in this state in the first place,' Nick began angrily. 'You really are—'

'Look, I'm back now,' Jemima cut in wearily—obviously having heard all of this, or something very like it, from Nick earlier today. Probably on their drive from the airport... 'I'm sorry if Jessica has been a nuisance—'

'The baby isn't the one at fault here, Gemini, and you know it,' Nick rasped furiously. 'You—'

'Could I suggest you continue to argue this out between the two of you once I've gone to bed?' Gemini felt sick now, as well as having this painful throbbing in her head.

Nick moved forward to grasp her arm. 'I'm coming with you,' he told her grimly. 'Jemima.' He turned to her briefly. 'Get your things together while I'm gone. I don't want to be away from home for any longer than I need to be when Gemini is feeling like this.'

Gemini was sure this last had to have been added for the benefit of Mrs James—because Nick wasn't fooling any of the rest of them with his concern. And as for how long he was away from home—it was totally irrelevant; the damage had been done now.

Jemima moved forward, kissing Gemini warmly on the cheek. 'I hope you feel better soon.' She smiled encouragingly. 'And, despite what Nick says—' she shot him an impatient glance '——I really am grateful to you for looking after Jessica for me.'

'She's a beautiful baby,' Gemini returned non-committally before turning to leave.

Nick continued to keep that firm hold on her arm as the two of them walked up the wide staircase together, and although Gemini was aware of his searching gaze on her she didn't acknowledge it by so much as a glance in his direction.

She felt like the casualty of some war, bruised inside as well as out. All she wanted was the peace of her bedroom. She wanted the numbness of sleep too, but she had a feeling that was going to be denied her...

'Hugh seems to feel there's more wrong with you than just a headache.' Nick was finally the one to softly break the awkward silence between them.

A sick heart didn't count as a genuine illness! 'Hugh fusses,' she dismissed impatiently. But she would have to have a few words with her assistant when next she saw him; she did not want him discussing her with Nick, no matter how much he might like and respect the older man.

'He cares, Gemini,' Nick corrected pointedly.

She didn't care what Hugh did, as long as he hadn't mentioned Danny's telephone call to the salon yesterday lunchtime!

Nick looked at her intently. 'You aren't feeling this way because of last night, are you? I didn't hurt you, did I?'

She was glad they had reached her bedroom as he asked these probing questions; she felt slightly weak at the knees again as she too easily recalled the passion between them.

She sat down heavily on the stool in front of her dressing table. 'Don't be ridiculous, Nick; I'm not made of porcelain,' she snapped irritably. 'But I would really rather not discuss last night,' she added weakly.

His mouth twisted derisively as he looked down at her.

'So I gathered earlier today,' he acknowledged dryly. 'But it's my experience that it isn't always possible to dismiss a moment of madness as easily as that!'

Was that what last night had been for them? A moment of madness...?

Or was he talking about something else, possibly referring to the existence of Jessica. Because if he was, he was going to have to give her a darn sight better explanation than that for having renewed his relationship with Jemima!

'You could be pregnant, Gemini,' Nick pointed out harshly as she made no response to his earlier remark. 'Unless you were using some sort of contraception—because I certainly wasn't!'

Pregnant...!

Over the weekend, while looking after Jessica, she had half dreamed of having Nick's child, of caring for their own child in the way she was for Jessica. But after today, after realising that Jessica was Nick's daughter, having his child herself was the last thing she wanted!

And what did he mean, unless *she* was using some sort of contraception? Most forms of contraception on her part he would surely have been aware of, and for her to have been on an oral contraception would have required premeditation on her part. Or another reason—another man!—she was taking oral contraception for!

God, they weren't back to Danny again—were they...?

'Oh, no, you don't, Nick.' She stood up shakily, facing him angrily. 'You aren't turning last night around on me. As I remember it, it was a mutual thing. And I'm not pregnant!' she assured him, with more force than certainty.

His expression became stony, and he stepped back. 'In that case this conversation is unnecessary,' he told her woodenly.

'Totally,' she agreed vehemently.

'Fine,' he acknowledged tautly.

But he made no move to leave…

'Wasn't it lucky for Jemima that you were at home earlier when she called from the airport to say she was back?' Gemini added challengingly.

'Very.' He nodded abruptly. 'If you recall, I wanted to be out to lunch with you,' he reminded her quietly.

So he had. So Nick being able to collect Jemima from the airport had just been coincidence, after all…

But that still didn't change anything. Not Jessica's parentage. Not Nick's involvement with Jemima. It certainly didn't make what had happened between the two of them last night any easier to come to terms with.

Gemini sighed tiredly. 'Jemima is waiting for you to take her home,' she reminded him flatly.

'She can damn well—' Nick broke off his forceful explosion, breathing deeply to calm his anger, shaking his head as he looked across at Gemini. 'Jemima's wants and needs aren't of particular importance to me at this moment.'

Because he was angry with her for just going off and leaving Jessica in that way. But it was an anger he would get over. As he had obviously got over being angry with Jemima for her affair with Danny last year…

'Forget about Jemima for the moment.' Much as she had realised earlier how much she still loved her twin, at this moment Gemini wished she could forget about Jemima for ever! 'Jessica is the innocent in all of this—mess,' she bit out distastefully. 'In my opinion, she is the one everyone ought to be thinking about.' And to her way of thinking Jessica would benefit from the presence in her life of both her parents!

Nick shook his head. 'Do you think I haven't talked to Jemima about that? But you know what she's like,' he added grimly before Gemini could formulate an answer. 'If she has to, she says she'll manage on her own.'

Gemini swallowed hard, her throat feeling very dry, her

lips hardly moving as she spoke. 'And does she have to?' She held her breath as she waited for his answer.

He sighed heavily. 'I don't think that's up to me—do you?' He looked at her intently.

Then who *was* it up to? Her? Was Nick—? No, not just Nick, but Jemima too. Were they expecting her to be the one to free Nick from his marriage? She couldn't! It wasn't fair of them to expect her to.

'You really do need to get into bed.' Nick easily noted the way her face had paled even more, leaving her chalky white now. 'As I said, I won't be long—'

'And as I said,' she put in firmly, no longer looking at him as she threw back the bedclothes, 'I shall be asleep when you get back.' She turned to look at him challengingly.

'Gemini…!' Nick groaned achingly. 'I wish to God I could make this easier for you—'

'Just go, Nick!' she bit out gratingly, having no idea how much longer she could hold onto the small reservoir of control she had left. 'Maybe—maybe later on we can talk like two civilised adults.' Although in her case it would have to be a lot later!

'I wish— Oh, damn what I wish,' he rasped harshly. 'But one thing, Gemini—I'm not going to apologise for what happened last night!' he told her grimly, before turning on his heel and slamming out of the room.

Gemini sat down gratefully on the bed. No one, it appeared, was going to apologise for last night…

A sob caught in the back of her throat, choking her, and she buried her face in her hands.

It was over, that rosy glow of hope she had lived under for the last six months, since she'd realised that she had unknowingly fallen in love with Nick. There was nowhere for those emotions to go now, no way she could even fight to keep Nick—not when there was a baby's welfare involved.

But it seemed that Nick and Jemima were leaving it to her to be the one who made any decisions that needed to be made. And, in the circumstances, there was only one decision that could be made.

Divorce...

Just the word made her shudder. How much more painful would the reality of it be, especially when she still loved Nick?'' How could she release him so that he could be with her sister? But, in the circumstances, how could she not...?

It was odd how calm she felt—well, perhaps calm was the wrong word, Gemini acknowledged ruefully to herself; resigned was probably the right way to describe how she felt.

She hadn't gone to sleep after she'd heard Nick leave the house with Jemima, but had lain awake, going over each of the options still open to her: to stay, to go, or to go with her dignity, at least, still intact. She had decided, finally, on the latter. Dignity, after all, was *all* she would be able to leave with!

That decision made, she *had* slept, heavily and deeply, waking to find the house in darkness, knowing that it must be some hours now since Nick had left with Jemima. And since he had returned...?

There was only one way to find that out, she realised as she looked at the bedside clock and saw it was an hour before their customary dinnertime; she would have to go downstairs and find out.

But before going downstairs she took a shower, washing her hair too, and after drying it, she brushed it until it shone in silky darkness about her shoulders. The make-up she applied hid the shadows beneath the blue of her eyes, her blusher giving colour to her cheeks and the red lipgloss she applied to her lips the exact colour of the red knee-length dress she chose to wear.

Her mother had told her years ago, 'If you know you're about to lose a fight, then make sure you're looking your best when you do it—it will make you feel better about yourself, and your opponent will at least take a second look!' It was too late for Nick to take a second look at her—he had already chosen the twin he wanted!—but it wasn't too late to follow her mother's advice and at least feel better about herself.

She was twenty-nine years of age, and although at this moment she might feel as if her life were over, she knew that in reality it wasn't. GemStone would still go on, and along with it so would she. Maybe not as she had been, but nevertheless she would go on.

Now all she had to do was get through this evening with Nick!

All…!

Maybe he wouldn't be downstairs, after all. No, of course he would be downstairs; he had said he wouldn't be long taking Jemima back home, and Nick wasn't yet a man who didn't keep his word. Yet? No matter what might have gone wrong between them now, Nick had always been honest with her. Or at least she had thought he had…

He was home. She could see the lamps on in the sitting-room as she came down the stairs, could even hear the chink of ice in his glass as he enjoyed his customary glass of whisky before dinner.

She drew in a deep breath, composing herself before she had to go in and face him. Composing herself! Was there *any* way to prepare herself for the encounter ahead?

'Gemini—!' Nick rose sharply to his feet as she appeared in the doorway. He was still wearing the dark green shirt and black trousers he'd changed into earlier this afternoon, and from the look of his hair he'd run his fingers through it several times while he sat and drank his whisky.

'Good evening, Nick,' she heard herself greet him smoothly as she strolled into the room. 'Could I have a glass of sherry, please?' she requested, before sitting down in the chair opposite him.

He didn't move, looking at her with narrowed eyes, his gaze searching. 'Is that wise, after your migraine earlier?' he said slowly.

'I feel fine now,' she dismissed.

'But—'

'Nick, I think I'm old enough to decide whether or not I feel well enough to drink a glass of sherry before dinner,' she told him derisively.

He gave an acknowledging inclination of his head before standing up. 'You seem to be old enough to decide quite a lot of things today,' he drawled dryly, moving to pour the sherry. 'Are there any other decisions you've made today that I should know about?' He quirked dark brows at her enquiringly as he gave her the glass of sherry.

Gemini drew in a deep breath, opening her mouth to speak—only to find she couldn't get a word past her lips!

Tell him, she instructed herself firmly. Go on, tell him you'll agree to the divorce. Go on, *tell* him!

'I've been asleep most of the afternoon, Nick,' she answered dismissively. 'I very rarely make decisions in my sleep.' She took a sip of the sherry, relieved when the alcohol burnt the back of her throat. It showed her she really was awake, and not in the middle of a nightmare!

He drew in a sharp breath. 'You certainly seem to be fully recovered,' he bit out tersely.

Her mouth twisted ruefully. 'Don't I just?' She took another sip of her sherry, its sustaining warmth helping slightly. But only slightly...

They were already behaving like strangers. Not even par-

ticularly polite ones, she realised sadly. And she knew a
lot of that was her fault. But she didn't feel particularly
polite!

'I told Mrs James that I didn't think you would be down
for dinner.' Nick frowned. 'I had better go and tell her I
was wrong.'

'No, I'll go.' Gemini stood up smoothly. 'After all, I'm
the one causing the inconvenience.' She was also the one
who needed a little breathing space!

At least she managed to get out of the room without
letting Nick see how unnerved she really was. She'd know
this wasn't going to be easy, but actually being with Nick,
looking at him, made it virtually impossible to come out
with the words she needed—had!—to say.

'Mrs Drummond!' The housekeeper looked pleased to
see her, at least, turning from the salad she had been preparing to smile at Gemini warmly. 'Are you feeling better?'

'Much,' Gemini lied. 'I just wanted to let you know I'm
down for dinner, too.'

Rachel James smiled. 'I would have brought you up a
tray, anyway.'

She was going to miss the other woman when she left,
Gemini realised sadly as she made her way slowly back to
the sitting-room. And she *would* be the one that left.

This had been Nick's home long before the two of them
were married; it was only right he should continue to live
here. Besides, there was a small, unoccupied apartment at
the back of the salon where she could go until she found
somewhere more suitable for her to live.

Suitable... She had a feeling that nowhere that Nick
wasn't would ever be that to her!

'That's fine,' she told him brightly as she came back into
the sitting-room, picking up her glass of sherry but not
sitting down this time; they would be going through to
dinner soon, anyway. 'Did Jemima get—home okay?' She

wasn't even sure where her sister's home was any more, although she knew that the one bed-roomed apartment where Jemima had used to live couldn't possibly be big enough for her, Jessica, and the baby's nanny.

Nick had resumed his seat beside the unlit fireplace, his expression becoming grim at the mention of her sister. 'Yes,' he confirmed tersely.

She nodded. 'It seems—very quiet without Jessica, doesn't it?' she realised wistfully.

It was strange how in only a matter of days a baby became the very centre of a household. Every move made, it seemed had been around the baby's needs.

Yes, she was going to miss Jessica. But once Jemima and Nick were actually together Gemini knew she would never be able to see her niece again. Basically because she would never be able to cope with seeing Nick and her sister together!

'Very,' Nick acknowledged tersely. 'Although look on the bright side. It means you'll be able to get back to living normally again.'

Normal. She wasn't sure what that was going to be for her in future...

But once again she had been given the ideal opportunity to say what needed to be said. Except...

This was probably her last evening with Nick. And it wasn't as if it was an especially relaxing evening, she inwardly rebuked herself. The two of them were like fencing opponents, circling around each other—although in their particular case neither of them seemed to want to strike that fatal blow!

She was being silly. Why make this more difficult for herself than it need be? Besides, she didn't feel in the least like eating, so why prolong the inevitable by drawing attention to her lack of appetite?

Mrs James stood in the doorway to announce happily, 'Dinner is ready.'

And with that Gemini had once again lost her chance, having little choice but to stand up and follow Nick into the dining-room, where their plates of melon and parma ham were already on the table.

'You seem very—subdued this evening.' Nick was the one to finally break the silence between them as they ate. 'Are you sure you're feeling completely well again after your migraine?'

'Positive,' she answered unhesitatingly.

And, despite her not feeling hungry, the melon and ham was actually giving her back some of her inner strength, reminding her that she hadn't eaten anything at all today but the croissants Mrs James had provided for her breakfast; she'd missed out on lunch altogether after refusing Nick's invitation. No wonder she had ended up with a migraine!

'Don't worry about me, Nick,' she told him dismissively. 'Like Jemima, I can look after myself.' Her mouth twisted wryly at her unintended mention of her sister; she just couldn't seem to keep Jemima out of the conversation. Although, in the circumstances, was that so surprising?

'But unlike Jemima,' Nick bit out abruptly, 'you don't have to!'

She looked at him over the rim of her wine glass, her eyes deeply blue. 'Don't I?' she challenged softly.

'No,' he returned harshly. 'You're my wife—'

'That's something I think we need to talk about—don't you?' she cut in firmly—before she lost her nerve!

They could carry on fencing the conversation like this all evening, and in the end the outcome would still be the same. Inevitably the same...

Nick's mouth had tightened grimly. 'I don't think I'm going to like what you have to say next!'

Gemini swallowed hard; she didn't like it, either—but one of them had to say it! And it had to be her...

'I'm leaving you, Nick,' she stated bluntly, stiffening in trepidation as she saw the pupils of Nick's eyes almost totally obscure the emerald iris.

CHAPTER TEN

'NOT NOW, Mrs James,' Nick rasped, looking over Gemini's shoulder to the doorway, where the housekeeper had appeared obviously to remove their used plates. 'I'll ring for you when we've finished,' he added gratingly.

Gemini didn't move, not giving so much as a glance in the other woman's direction. But she still knew the exact moment the housekeeper left to return to the kitchen as she suddenly felt the full blast of Nick's furious gaze levelled in her own direction.

'I told you Sunday night,' he bit out chillingly. 'I'll never agree to an easy divorce so that you can marry my brother!'

Gemini shook her head. 'The question of divorce is up to you, Nick.' She wasn't going to make all of this easy for him, either; he could do some of the work himself! 'I merely want you to know that I'm leaving.'

Merely...! This physical letting go was the hardest thing she had ever done in her life. She was sure the emotional letting go was going to be so much harder.

A nerve pulsed in his rigidly clenched jaw. 'I think you're a fool. You know that, don't you?' he bit out coldly.

She gave a choked laugh. 'I think I'm a fool, too, Nick,' she said self-derisively—she was a fool ever to have thought Nick might one day love her! 'But sometimes our choices are—limited by other people.'

And in this case he and Jemima hadn't given her a choice!

'I've already told you that Danny is—living with something else,' he reminded her tautly.

She sighed at the way he constantly returned to his

brother. 'My decision isn't based on anything Danny is or isn't doing,' she told Nick flatly. 'I'm doing this for me.' And an innocent baby who, in Gemini's opinion, didn't deserve either of the parents she had been given!

He looked at her searchingly for several minutes, and then he sighed heavily. 'I see,' he acknowledged flatly. 'There's no arguing with that, is there?'

'No,' she confirmed firmly. No amount of arguing, or anything else for that matter, on Nick's part, would change her mind now.

'Where will you go?' He looked at her with narrowed eyes.

She gave an indulgent laugh. 'I do have friends of my own, you know, Nick!'

'I know you do,' he bit out impatiently. 'I just—I don't like to think of you—out there, on your own.'

'Out where?' she scorned. 'I lived on my own for twenty-eight years, Nick; I'm used to it.' Although after living her with Nick for over a year she knew she was going to find it much harder to be on her own now...

'I suppose you are,' he acknowledged with a sigh. 'I just—I never thought it would actually come to this, Gemini.' He looked at her regretfully.

She raised dark brows. 'I don't think either of us did, Nick—otherwise there would have been no point in our marrying each other in the first place!' She reached out her hand to touch him as he sat across the table from her. Instantly she realised what she was doing, and quickly withdrew it again, clasping her hands together beneath the table; she mustn't do that again. To touch Nick could be her undoing. 'But sometimes—events change things,' she added dully. And Jessica's parentage had certainly changed things for her.

'Gemini, there's no reason for you to move out until you have somewhere else to go—'

'Oh, I think there is,' she cut in determinedly. If she didn't leave now she might weaken in her resolve, and that would only complicate things even more.

Nick's mouth twisted. 'Much as I found last night—enjoyable, I'm not about to force myself on you if you stay, Gemini.'

'I didn't think you were.' Heated colour warmed her cheeks at the remembrance of their lovemaking. 'I just don't think it's a good idea.' Because *she* might force herself on him!

Strangely, nothing had had happened in the last twenty-four hours had changed her love for him, and if her rival weren't her own sister, who had borne him a child, then Gemini knew she might have still tried to fight for her husband. But she knew Nick well enough to realise that if he had become involved with Jemima again, then he must obviously love her. And that was something it was impossible to fight any more.

'He won't be there for you, you know, Gemini,' Nick told her grimly. 'He's never been there for anyone but himself,' he added bitterly.

'If we're talking about Danny again,' she scorned dismissively, 'then I already know that!'

'Of course we're talking about Danny!' Nick stood up forcefully, moving away from the dining-table to stand in front of the window looking out—although Gemini was sure he saw nothing of their garden outside, his thoughts all inwards. 'Gemini, there are things about Danny that I think you should know—'

'I'm not interested, Nick,' she assured him lightly. 'I've already told you that Danny, and what happened in the past, makes no difference to me now. I—I just know I have to follow my heart. And my heart tells me that our marriage is unfair to everyone concerned,' she added emotionally. 'I know that neither of us ever meant to hurt the other, Nick.'

She looked across at him with tear-wet eyes as he turned back to face her. 'But, nevertheless, we've done so. It's time all that hurt and deceit was put to an end,' she added determinedly.

His shoulders slumped. 'Perhaps you're right. I-I'm going to miss you, Gemini,' he told her gruffly.

He was going to miss *her*? She felt as if her heart were being physically wrenched from her chest! But through all the pain she kept seeing Jessica's trusting face, and she knew that no matter how it hurt to walk away from Nick she was doing the right thing.

She gave a strained smile. 'You'll soon get used to it, Nick. Within a few weeks it will be as if I was never here.' Especially if Jemima moved in here with the baby!

His mouth tightened. 'I doubt that very much,' he bit out sharply.

Maybe the memory of last night might be a little difficult to forget, for both of them—there was no denying it had been beautiful—but the rest of their marriage would quickly fade. Until last night there had been nothing momentous to remember!

Gemini stood up, walking gracefully across the room until she stood only feet away from Nick. 'I hope we can part as friends, Nick?' She looked across at him searchingly. Not even to have his friendship would just be too much for her to bear!

He reached out to clasp the tops of her arms, pulling her close to him, resting her head against his shoulder as his arms moved about her and held her protectively close. 'I'll always be here for you, Gemini,' he assured her huskily. 'No matter what happens.'

For a while, maybe he would, but the time had come for him to choose between the two sisters—and Gemini was taking herself out of the picture. But as long as she knew

Nick didn't hate her, maybe she would be able to cope with never seeing him again.

Maybe...

For the moment she just revelled in being held in his arms, the beat of his heart sounding as loudly as her own. God, how she wished—

She pulled firmly away from him, forcing another strained smile to her lips before reaching up to kiss him on one side of his rigidly clenched jaw. 'We're being extremely civilised, Nick,' she teased lightly.

'Civilised!' he repeated disgustedly, his hands painful on her arms as he grasped her painfully this time. 'I would like to break someone's neck!'

She arched dark brows. 'Mine?' she offered helpfully.

'No,' he snapped impatiently, although he shook her slightly. 'I never intended to let you go, Gemini,' he muttered grimly. 'When you mentioned divorce to me the other night, I—I determined I would never let it happen. But I realise now there's nothing I can do to stop it, is there?' he asked heavily.

'No,' she acknowledged softly.

'No,' he acknowledged harshly. 'But I can kiss you once more. Don't stop me, Gemini,' he warned as she stiffened guardedly. 'At this moment you're still my wife, and I—I—' He didn't finish his sentence; instead his mouth came crashing down on hers.

Gemini became fluid in his arms, her own arms up about his neck as she returned the kiss. His savagery quickly turned to searing passion, his hands moving restlessly up and down her spine as he curved her into him.

For Gemini it was heaven. Nothing else mattered in that moment except to be in Nick's arms, being kissed by him as if he never wanted to stop.

But several moments later that was exactly what he did, wrenching his mouth from hers to look down at her with dark eyes. 'Remember, Gemini,' he bit out gratingly. 'I'm always here.'

'Always is a long time, Nick,' she returned gruffly.

He nodded abruptly. 'A lifetime.'

She gave a rueful smile, shaking her head as she moved away from him, suddenly bereft at the loss of his warmth, but knowing she didn't dare stay close to him any longer. If she did, she would break down completely, promise him anything if she could be the one he loved. But it wasn't just her dignity she wanted to keep; she had to keep her pride too. Most of all, she knew Nick wouldn't thank her for putting him in such a position.

'Apologise to Mrs James for me, will you? I don't think I could manage to eat any more dinner,' she told Nick self-derisively. 'I'll just go upstairs and pack a few things to take with me—'

'You're going now?' Nick rasped disbelievingly. 'Right this minute?'

She nodded abruptly. 'I think it best, don't you?' she dismissed. 'Then if you don't mind, I'll come back and collect the rest of my things one day this week while you're at work?'

He stepped back, thrusting his hands into his trouser pockets. 'If that's what you want to do,' he accepted harshly.

She nodded again. 'You'll warn Mrs James about my visit later in the week?'

Nick looked as if he were about to make a blistering reply to this comment, and then thought better of it. 'As I have no intention of telling Mrs James you've left me, I suggest you tell her,' he bit out tautly. 'Or just use your key,' he added impatiently.

Gemini swallowed hard at his unmistakable bitterness. Separations, even when there was no love involved—at least, not on one side!—were always hard, it seemed. 'I'll be leaving my house key behind when I go this evening. Be sensible, Nick,' she continued determinedly as he would have protested. 'It's hardly the thing to do to let your ex-wife keep a key to the house; I could just walk in at any time unannounced!'

The green of his eyes was as hard and cold as the stone they resembled. 'I doubt you'll ever walk in here on anything you shouldn't,' he returned disparagingly.

That depended on how one looked at it, Gemini decided. To come here and find Nick and Jemima, along with Jessica, playing at happy families, would be totally unacceptable to her, even if it couldn't be classed that way by Nick!

'And you aren't my ex-wife,' Nick added hardily.

'Yet,' she accepted ruefully.

He shrugged. 'You pick you own time, your own reasons. I want no part of it.'

There was plenty of time to talk of divorce. The fact that she wasn't married to Jessica's father didn't seem to have bothered Jemima so far, so it probably wouldn't now, either. Better to wait until all emotions were settled before talking of it again. If they ever were settled!

'I—I'll go and pack some of my things, then, and be on my way.' Gemini hesitated at the dining-room door, knowing that once she stepped out of this room, ended this conversation, everything was over between Nick and herself.

'Do what you like,' Nick rasped. 'I'm sure you're going to anyway!' he added as he turned away to stare out of the window once again.

Gemini took in everything about him in that last lingering glance; the dark thickness of his hair as it rested on his shirt collar, the muscled width of his shoulders, hunched slightly now as he kept his hands buried in his pockets, leanly tapered waist, powerful thighs and long, muscular legs.

She loved everything about him. Didn't doubt for a moment that she was going to love him for as long as she lived!

'"Who's been sleeping in my bed?" said Baby Bear,' Hugh muttered irritably from behind her.

Gemini glanced up from the design she had been working on, her face paling slightly as she saw the photograph of Nick and herself on their wedding day that Hugh held in one of his large hands—a photograph that had stood on the small table beside her bed in the adjoining apartment until a few minutes ago!

'I went next door to collect some material from the store,' he explained dismissively. 'Now, are you going to tell me what's going on?' he prompted impatiently as she made no response.

She swallowed hard, affecting a shrug. 'Surely it's obvious?' she returned lightly.

'It's obvious you slept in the apartment last night,' Hugh accepted. 'What's not obvious—at least, not to me!—is why?'

Gemini shrugged. 'I've left Nick,' she stated bluntly.

'Left Nick…' Hugh repeated softly. 'Left him as in—'

'As in *left him*, Hugh,' she cut in sharply. After a night spent silently weeping as she lay in the bed in the adjoining apartment, her mood was not at its best! 'We're going to be divorced,' she added, so that there should be no lingering doubt in Hugh's mind as to exactly what she meant.

Hugh sank slowly down onto the chair opposite her own at the table they worked on. 'I don't believe it,' he muttered incredulously.

Gemini shrugged. 'You said it yourself earlier this week. I'm not happy. And neither is Nick,' she added firmly as he would have protested. 'In the circumstances, the best thing for us to do is part. And, in the fullness of time, we'll be divorced.'' If she kept saying it, maybe one day she would be able to accept that that was the fate of her marriage to Nick!

Hugh shook his head. 'And what does Nick think of all this?'

She gave a shaky laugh at the question. 'He's in agreement with it, of course,' she dismissed.

'I don't see any ''of course'' about it.' Hugh shook his head grimly.

'He's agreed to it, okay?' Gemini told him impatiently. Talking about this did not make it any easier to bear!

'But it isn't his idea, is it?' Hugh guessed triumphantly. 'Gemini, what—?'

'Hugh, I appreciate your concern, and I love you very much, but I really think this is between Nick and myself,' she told him firmly, blue eyes looking across at him in challenge.

'Okay, I accept that,' Hugh nodded grimly. 'But I care about you both, and—' He broke off as the salon door opened with a crash, having swung forcefully back on its hinges and hit the wall behind. 'Nick...?' he greeted him questioningly.

The reason for Hugh's uncertainty about the identity of their visitor soon became obvious to Gemini as she turned towards the door; most of the person who had entered so noisily was obscured by the biggest bouquet of flowers she had ever seen!

Her heart sank at the fact that it probably was Nick behind those fragrant blooms. She hadn't expected to see him again so soon—if at all! And certainly not carrying flowers...

She stood up slowly, the colour leaving her cheeks as she found herself looking at a furious Nick as he swung the bouquet away from his face, green eyes glittering coldly.

'Er—I think I'll take an early lunch.' Hugh excused himself, having taken one look at their faces before making the decision to make himself scarce. 'Catch up with you later, Nick,' he told the other man as he grabbed his jacket and left.

Gemini stared at Nick as he made no effort to move away from the doorway, the flowers still tightly gripped in his hands.

She shook her head. 'It's too late for flowers, Nick—'

'These aren't from me, damn it!' he assured her contemptuously, throwing the bouquet down disgustedly on a table beside him. 'But I would appreciate your telling Danny I do not want him sending my wife flowers to our home ever again!' he added caustically, his gaze scathing as it raked over her. 'Obviously you haven't managed to contact him yet to tell him that you've left me!' He strode forward to move restlessly around the room.

Gemini moved too, a puzzled frown marring her brow as she pulled the envelope off the top of the bouquet, opening it up to take the card out from inside and read the message written there.

'Do you have any idea how I felt when those were delivered to the house this morning?' Nick turned to attack her, his hands clenched tightly at his sides. 'It's one thing knowing about the two of you. Quite another to have your relationship thrust down my throat by having Danny send you flowers—'

'They're from Jemima, Nick,' she cut in quietly, holding out the card to him so that he could read it. 'To thank me for looking after Jessica.' And in the circumstances, the flowers—even though they were beautiful lilies—were most unwelcome!

He frowned down at the card, closing his eyes briefly before turning away. 'How the hell was I supposed to know that?' he muttered angrily. 'After what happened yesterday, it was only natural to assume the flowers had to be from Danny.'

He felt foolish now, Gemini realised, and understandably so, but... 'I've already told you that my decision to leave has nothing to do with Danny—'

'And I'm really supposed to believe that?' Nick scorned. 'After his telephone call over the weekend?'

'I've explained all that,' she sighed. 'I've also tried to explain that there is absolutely no reason why Danny should send me flowers—ever!' she added vehemently.

Nick looked at her with narrowed eyes. 'Where did you stay last night, Gemini?' he prompted hardily.

She shrugged; it certainly wasn't any secret, not if Hugh knew about it! 'Here.' She watched as Nick looked about them disbelievingly. 'The apartment next door,' she explained dryly.

Nick became very still, glaring across at her. 'And I spent most of last night trying very hard to make sense of why you left, Gemini,' he bit out abruptly, shaking his head. 'I realise the fact that we have been to bed together changes things slightly. But you weren't even willing to sit and talk about it.'

'I told you, there's nothing left to say,' she said woodenly, still not willing to discuss the night they had spent together; it was just too painful.

'And if I disagree?' he challenged.

She shrugged. 'I'm not answerable for what you think or feel, Nick—'

'Yes, you are, damn you!' His face twisted angrily. 'Monday night I actually began to think—to hope. Hell, you made sure you left me with none of that hope when you left last night!'

Because his responsibilities lay elsewhere! Why didn't he stop this? Why make things more difficult than they needed to be?

She shook her head. 'Because if I had thought there was room for any of that hope then I wouldn't have left in the first place,' she told him. 'Can't you see how difficult you're making this, Nick? For both of us?'

'I would like to make it so difficult for you that you can't go through with it!' he snapped harshly.

Gemini sighed. 'Then you obviously have no idea of what I went through to make the decision in the first place!' she returned vehemently. 'Now, I have been more than fair with you, Nick—'

'Fair!' he repeated disgustedly. 'I'm not interested in *fair*. I'm interested in having my wife back home where she belongs!' He glared at her.

'Bullying me won't achieve that, Nick,' she assured him flatly.

'Neither has reasoning. Or seduction,' he added reluctantly.

Her chin rose defensively. 'And what does that tell you?' she bit out sharply.

'It tells me you're too damned stubborn for your own good!' His eyes glittered dangerously.

Gemini shook her head, her smile completely lacking in humour. 'It didn't even take twenty-four hours, did it? For anger to take over from the friendship we offered each other before we parted last night,' she explained heavily at his questioning look.

His hands clenched and unclenched at his sides. 'I want to be your friend, Gemini,' he told her huskily. 'I just—I think it might take a while,' he admitted ruefully.

She sighed. 'Take as long as you like, Nick; I don't intend going anywhere. Now, if you wouldn't mind, I have some work to do. And I'm sure you have some things of your own to do,' she added pointedly. If he had been at the house this morning, when the flowers arrived, then he obviously hadn't been to see Jemima yet.

He gave a grimace of a smile. 'Unlike you, I haven't felt in the mood for work today.' His casual black denims and pale cream shirt were evidence of that. 'Although you're probably right; I should check in with Karen and see if there's anything urgent at the office that needs my attention,' he added thoughtfully.

That wasn't quite what she had meant by 'things' he had to do, but if it meant he was leaving now, that would do for a start!

'Hugh should be back soon,' she managed conversationally as he made no effort to leave.

Nick gave a grimace of a smile. 'Don't worry, Gemini; my bullying tactics are over for today!'

She felt the heat in her cheeks. 'I didn't mean—'

'Yes, you did,' he derided mockingly. 'And you're probably right.' He shook his head. 'I'm just not used to losing, Gemini,' he added self-disgustedly.

Was that why he had renewed his relationship with Jemima? Because he hadn't been able to accept, fifteen months ago, that she preferred his younger brother?

Whatever his reasons for doing that, it was the reason he was going to lose now, with her!

Her mouth twisted derisively. 'Then don't think of it as losing, Nick; just think of it as regaining what you really want!'

'And how do you know what I want?' he grated, eyes narrowed once again.

Gemini shrugged. 'Do any of us really know that, even about ourselves?'

His mouth tightened. 'Obviously not,' he bit out tautly, walking towards the door. 'I'm sorry about the flowers.' He looked down at them, the delicate blooms having taken a bit of a battering from his rough handling of them earlier. 'I hope you manage to salvage them.'

Gemini didn't even intend trying to do that; the flowers

were beautiful, but they were also from her sister—and she didn't want any reminders of Jemima around her at the moment, either!

'Don't worry about it,' she dismissed. 'I'm certainly not going to,' she added hardily.

Nick nodded, hesitating by the door. 'You—take care, Gemini.' He'd obviously thought better of what he had originally been about to say.

She gave a slight inclination of her head. 'You too.'

She managed to hold onto her self-control until the door closed behind him, and then she sank down like a deflated balloon. This was awful. Terrible. And it was nowhere near over yet.

The truth of that became apparent an hour later—when Jemima herself walked in to the studio!

Was this nightmare never going to end? Gemini asked herself as she looked across at her sister. Probably not, she inwardly conceded; after all, she was very much awake!

'Jessica!' Hugh, who had returned from his lunch half an hour ago, got excitedly to his feet to rush over and take the baby from Jemima's arms.

Gemini raised her eyes heavenwards. 'I think everyone has gone mad!' she muttered as her fifteen-stone male assistant murmured baby talk to the entranced Jessica.

Jemima laughed huskily as she too watched Hugh's antics.

'Babies have that effect on people!'

Jemima looked more relaxed herself today, Gemini noted. Her sister's obvious tiredness of yesterday must have been solved by a good night's sleep. Although Gemini couldn't help wondering how Jemima had achieved that, with Jessica to look after during the night.

Or maybe her sister's happily relaxed demeanour could be attributed to another reason. After all, Nick *had* left an hour ago...

CHAPTER ELEVEN

GEMINI drew herself up stiffly. 'What can I do for you, Jemima?' she prompted abruptly.

After all, this was her place of work—and just recently it was turning into nothing more than a meeting place!

Jemima turned back from watching indulgently as Hugh played with Jessica. 'I— Oh, you received the lilies!' she realised happily as she saw the blooms in a vase on the table near the door. 'I know they've always been your favourite flower.'

They had, but after today that was no longer the case...! And the only reason the flowers hadn't already been consigned to the bin was because Hugh had been horrified at the thought of throwing them away and had promised to take them home with him.

'Although I thought I sent them to the house,' Jemima added in a puzzled voice.

'You did,' Gemini dismissed briskly. 'Nick brought them over for me earlier.'

'That was nice of him.' Her sister nodded, sitting down on the edge of Gemini's work-table. 'Hugh, I don't suppose you would like to do me a favour, would you?' She smiled across the room at him engagingly.

He looked up from the baby, his mouth twisting derisively as he saw straight through the deliberate charm of that smile. 'If it involves Jessica, no problem.' He shrugged. 'Anything else and the answer is no,' he told her bluntly; there was no love lost between him and Gemini's twin sister.

'It involves Jessica,' Jemima assured him dryly. 'Would

you like to take her for a short walk? Go down to the chemist at the corner and buy some baby lotion for me? Her pushchair is outside,' she added helpfully.

Hugh looked across at Gemini with questioning eyes, obviously waiting for an opinion on this move before giving Jemima his answer.

In truth, Gemini didn't want him to leave; he was the only person in the room at the moment stopping the conversation between the two sisters deteriorating into verbal abuse. But, quite honestly, loving Nick as she did, Gemini had had it with being the polite victim in all of this. So if Jemima had come here to gloat—

'Please, go ahead, Hugh,' she told him brightly. 'And take your time,' she added encouragingly.

He nodded slowly, Jessica happily ensconced in his arms. 'Fine,' he accepted. 'Do you have the money for the lotion!' he prompted Jemima hardily.

Jemima laughed softly once Hugh had left with Jessica— and the money for the lotion. 'He really doesn't like me, does he?' she said ruefully.

'Not much,' Gemini confirmed uncaringly. 'Now, why are you here, Jemima?'

Her sister laughed again. 'What is it with everyone today?' She shook her head in puzzlement. 'I thought the two of us had resolved our—differences yesterday?'

Resolved their—! 'Don't be ridiculous, Jemima,' she dismissed. 'I looked after Jessica for you because you left me with no choice. I think, in the circumstances...' She swallowed hard as her voice shook emotionally. 'In the circumstances,' she repeated determinedly, 'it was the height of insensitivity on your part!'

'Oh.' Jemima grimaced. 'You're still mad at me, then?'

Still? She only found out about it yesterday, hardly time for her to have recovered from the shock, let alone get over her feelings of betrayal!

Gemini stood up agitatedly. 'Of course I'm still mad at you,' she answered impatiently. 'I always will be,' she added vehemently.

However much she might have found herself illogically pleased to see her twin again yesterday, the breach between them was actually wider now than it had ever been. And nothing would ever change that...

'But—' Jemima broke off, shaking her head. 'I came here to tell you my good news.' She sighed. 'I had hoped you would be happy for me,' she added wistfully.

Nick *had* seen her sister after he'd left here this morning! Which meant Jemima knew about their separation...

In that case, it didn't take too much imagination to realise what her sister's good news was...!

Gemini drew in a ragged breath. 'I hope you'll be happy together,' she said stiffly.

Her sister pulled a face. 'You don't sound very sincere,' she derided.

Gemini clenched her hands together in front of her. 'That's probably because at this moment I don't feel very sincere! How could you, Jemima?' she choked. 'How could either of you?' Tears glistened in the deep blue of her eyes.

'But, Gemini, it's been over a year now—' her sister protested frowningly.

'I know exactly how long it's been,' she cut in shakily. 'Just don't invite me to the wedding!' she added vehemently; knowing her sister as she did, that was exactly what she would do next!

Jemima shook her head dazedly. 'I don't understand this. I know the two of you were married rather quickly after you met, but you seemed happy enough with Nick when I saw you together yesterday...?'

'I was,' she confirmed tautly. 'I have been.'

Her sister shrugged. 'Then where's the problem?' She grimaced. 'Danny and I had both hoped—'

'What does Danny Drummond have to do with this?' Gemini cut in sharply.

Her sister's cheeks flushed prettily. 'He's asked me to marry him—and I've said yes,' she announced awkwardly.

Gemini stared at Jemima, totally dumbstruck. So Danny's effort to track her sister down over the weekend had paid off, and now Jemima was going to marry him?

Poor Nick, came her next thought. How on earth was he going to take the news that his brother had literally pipped him at the post a second time?

Jemima sighed. 'We've been going through a rough time of it lately. There's been faults on both sides,' she conceded heavily. 'But the truth of the mater is, no matter what problems we may had had in the past, I do love him and want to be with him very much,' she admitted clearly.

Gemini felt as if she were as immovable as a statue. She could barely think, let alone attempt to move. 'And what about Jessica?' she managed to get out through stiff lips.

Jemima smiled at the mention of her daughter. 'She and Danny adore each other.' She laughed softly.

Gemini didn't doubt it for a moment; she knew herself just how charming Danny could be. But where did all this leave Nick, Jessica's father...

'We had hoped that you and Nick would be our two witnesses at the wedding next month,' her sister explained ruefully.

No! The refusal screamed in her brain. It was bad enough that her sister had once again separated her from the man she loved; it would be impossible for her to go to the wedding and witness Nick's pain in losing Jemima a second time.

Gemini shook her head. 'I'm going on an extensive buying trip next month,' she answered stiffly.

Now it was Jemima's turn to look tearful. 'Gemini, I know we haven't been close for a while—and I know I

behaved badly in the past—but can't you see that everything turned out for the best in the end?' she added be-
seechingly. 'You and Nick were always much more suited
to each other than he and I were, and——Gemini, can't you
just be happy for me?'

'You're always so irresponsible, Jemima,' she told her
sister heavily. 'Do you ever stop to think how you're affecting other people's lives with your actions?'

'I'm starting to,' Jemima admitted huskily. 'This last
week brought it all home to me. I was so mad at Danny,
you see, for just taking off on his work without a thought
for how I was going to manage with my own work if he
didn't get back in time to look after Jessica. Which he
obviously didn't do.' She grimaced. 'So I left the baby with
Janey, with instructions for her to bring the baby to you if
Danny wasn't back by the weekend. I was so angry with
him! But once I got to the States I realised what a mistake
I had made. By which time I had involved you and Nick,
and it was too late to do anything about it.'

Gemini stared at her sister uncomprehendingly. None of
this made sense. What——?

Nick had told her that Danny had a woman living at his
apartment with him. Could that woman possibly be
Jemima? Was this one of the things about Danny that Nick
had thought she should know?

And if Jemima *had* been living with Danny all the
time——!

'Jemima,' she began slowly, moistening suddenly dry
lips, 'Who is Jessica's father?'

Her sister looked stunned by the question. 'Why, Danny
is, of course. You don't think I would have tried to palm
someone else's child off on him, do you?' she added indignantly. 'I know you don't have a very high opinion of
me, Gemini, but I think that's going a bit far!'

Gemini swallowed hard, unmoved by her sister's indignation; this was too important for her to care about Jemima's feelings at this moment! 'But to my knowledge you and Danny broke up over a year ago,' she reminded her probingly.

'That's true,' her sister acknowledged abruptly. 'We've fallen out half a dozen times more since then, too, but we still go back to each other. Danny and I have been living together since I found out about the baby eight months ago,' she added dismissively.

Danny was Jessica's father...

And Jessica had the green eyes of her uncle! Despite having brown eyes himself, Danny must carry the green-eyed gene!

And Danny and Jemima had been living together for eight months. Hence Danny's telephone calls over the weekend, when he'd returned home and tried to locate Jemima and his baby daughter. But he hadn't asked after Jessica, only Jemima, which was why Gemini hadn't mentioned her, either.

Oh, God, what had she done?

She sat down abruptly in one of the chairs, her face buried in her hands. She had thought—believed—

Nick's impatience with Jemima over the weekend, and again yesterday, when she'd finally come home, suddenly came back to Gemini. It hadn't been the impatience of an indulgent if irritated lover; he had genuinely been angry with Jemima for just leaving Jessica in the way that she had. And, if that were the case, then his concern for Gemini over the weekend had been genuine too...

As had his tenderness and passion when they'd made love two nights ago...

What had she done?

More to the point, what could she do about it now that she had done it?

From what her sister had just told her, Nick obviously

hadn't been having an affair with Jemima at all, and certainly wasn't Jessica's father—but how could Gemini possibly go to him and tell him she now knew that? Especially when he couldn't possibly realise she had ever thought that in the first place! She couldn't. That was the answer.

'Gemini...?' Her sister was looking across at her anxiously.

Gemini looked back at her blankly, lost in her own misery. Those conversations she had had with Nick over the last few days... He'd believed *she* was the one who was being unfaithful in their marriage. With Danny. And he had tried, in his own way, to shield her from being hurt all over again by Danny's continued relationship with Jemima.

Which must mean that Nick cared for her.

But did he care enough to take her back?

One thing she did know: she could never tell her sister of the mistaken assumptions she had made over the weekend. She could never tell anyone! Although she might have no choice, if she wanted to retrieve her marriage, but to explain his mistake to Nick...

The realisation made her face pale even more.

'Let me know when you have a specific date for the wedding,' she told her sister distractedly. 'I'll try to be there.'

Jemima stood up. 'But you won't be one of our witnesses?' she pressured.

If she hadn't sorted things out with Nick by then, it might be her only opportunity to see him again! If he should decide to go to the wedding...

'Ask me closer to the time,' she replied. 'And congratulations,' she added belatedly. 'Perhaps marriage will help the two of you feel more settled and secure with each other. I certainly think you're doing the right thing for Jessica,' she added warmly as she thought of her adorable niece.

Jemima nodded, looking towards the door as Hugh could

be heard returning with the baby. 'Will you—could you mention it to Nick, do you think?' she requested awkwardly. 'He didn't seem terribly pleased with me yesterday. And he and Danny haven't spoken for months.'

Which begged the question why ask Nick and herself to be their witnesses at all? But Gemini already knew the answer to that; she and Nick were Jemima and Danny's only relatives.

'I'll try,' she answered non-committally; after all, she wasn't sure when she would be talking to Nick again. Or how.

'Good enough.' Jemima squeezed her hand gratefully. 'It means a lot to Danny and myself,' she added, seconds before Hugh came in holding a sleeping Jessica.

Gemini wasn't sure whether to cry or laugh once her sister had left with the baby. Cry because she had left Nick for absolutely no reason. Laugh because now that the danger of Jemima had passed she felt slightly ridiculous in her assumptions. Jemima, for one, had been horrified that Gemini could possibly have thought Jessica was anyone else's daughter but Danny's. Thank goodness her sister hadn't realised she had thought Jessica was Nick's!

But what did she do now?

She'd left Nick for all the wrong reasons, but to tell him of the things she had thought about him concerning Jemima would surely only broaden the rift between them. She felt trapped between a rock and a hard place. And in neither direction did she stand to be reconciled with Nick...

'I thought you intended coming to collect your things when I was safely at work?' Nick rasped from her open bedroom doorway.

Gemini had heard his car in the driveway as he arrived home at the end of his working day, her hands shaking slightly at the realisation that she was about to come face to face with her husband for the first time in two days. It had taken her that long to pluck up the courage to come here!

And also to come up with a legitimate reason for seeing him at all!

It had been the longest two days of her life, when her emotions had seesawed between despair and hope. Despair because she thought she might have lost Nick for good. Hope because part of her so wanted Nick to care for her; she didn't believe he could have made love to her in the way he had if he didn't feel anything for her at all. And they *were* married to each other...

And so she'd decided to come to the house, ostensibly for more of her things, at a time she'd hoped Nick would be home—only to be informed by a still upset Mrs James that he had told her he would be late home this evening. The only answer to that, that Gemini could see, was that she would just have to linger over her packing for as long as possible.

Turning slowly to face Nick across the width of her bedroom, she saw he didn't look as if the last two days had been exactly happy ones for him either. His expression was grim, his face slightly thinner too, and those green eyes were narrowed warily.

He was wary! Gemini's knees were knocking together just at the sight of him, making her relieved that she had chosen to wear a deep blue trouser suit and cream blouse, the former hopefully hiding the fact that her legs were shaking from nervousness!

She had known many emotions with Nick—gratitude, indifference, friendship, love and then passion—but she couldn't actually remember ever feeling this emotionally frightened before... So much depended on this meeting. If they should argue again—!

But she was determined they wouldn't argue again. It would solve nothing and achieve even less.

'You don't mind, do you?' she asked huskily, holding up the gold brush set he had given her last Christmas that she had been about to put in the open suitcase on her bed.

'Take what you like,' he dismissed harshly, looking extremely remote in the dark business suit and white shirt he had worn to work. 'They're your things.'

Not very encouraging. Gemini grimaced inwardly. But then, what had she expected? Nick was a proud man, and she had walked out on him and their marriage; of course he was angry.

'Have you seen Danny?'

She turned sharply back to Nick, her gaze searching the grimness of his face but unable to read anything from his closed expression. 'Is this a trick question?' she finally replied warily.

He gave a humourless smile. 'Not at all,' he drawled mockingly. 'I merely wondered if there had been any—developments in that direction?' He arched dark brows.

A bubble of hysterical laughter welled up in her throat. Developments? Would he call the two of them being asked to be the witnesses at Jemima and Danny's wedding next month a 'development'?

She shrugged dismissively. 'Several, actually,' she drawled self-derisively. 'But I think we need to sit and talk about them in less—intimate surroundings.' She looked pointedly around the room that had been her own bedroom until three days ago. And would be again if she had her way!

'I—' Nick broke off as he heard the approach of the housekeeper in the hallway outside. 'Yes, Mrs James?' he prompted kindly as she appeared in the open doorway.

Rachel James looked awkwardly at the two of them. 'I—

wondered if Mrs Drummond would be staying for dinner?'
she prompted breathlessly, looking painfully at Gemini.

The other woman had been so upset when Gemini had
left on Tuesday, and was obviously still very shaken by the
separation. But there was nothing Gemini could say or do
to alleviate the other woman's obvious unhappiness with
the situation. Not when her own unhappiness was so over-
whelming!

Nick quirked dark brows at Gemini. 'I don't know—is
she?' he queered softly.

'I'm afraid not,' Gemini refused regretfully. 'Hugh and
Alan have invited me to have a meal with them this evening,' she explained, so that there would be no misunderstanding about the reason for her refusal.

Hugh had been badgering her all week to go and have a
meal with Alan and himself at their apartment. He seemed
determined to try and look after her—whether she wanted
to be looked after or not! She had finally given in and
accepted an invitation for tonight—she'd thought she might
need a little cheering up after collecting some of her things
from the house. She certainly hadn't thought she would
receive an invitation to dine with Nick!

'Just the one for dinner again, then, Mrs James,' Nick
told the housekeeper, waiting until the other woman had
left before turning back to Gemini. 'I had better let you get
on if you're going on to Hugh's.'

'I'm not expected for another half an hour,' Gemini put
in quickly, colour heating her cheeks as Nick raised questioning brows at her outburst. 'I do want—need to talk to
you, Nick,' she told him huskily. 'Just not here. I—'

'Have dinner with me tomorrow evening?' he put in suddenly. 'Not here,' he agreed grimly. 'I can pick you up at
the salon at say eight o'clock, and we can go on to a restaurant?'

Gemini looked at him searchingly. Was Nick actually

asking her out? Don't be stupid, Gemini, she instantly re-
monstrated with herself; she was the one who had said she
needed to talk to him, and a restaurant would be a natural
place for that conversation to take place.

She moistened dry lips. 'That sounds—fine,' she accepted gruffly.

Nick nodded abruptly, his closed expression giving away
nothing of how he felt at having his invitation accepted.
'Would you like to join me in a sherry before you go?' he
offered evenly.

Would she? She would like to join him for much more
than a pre-dinner drink! But if the sherry was all that was
on offer…!

'That would be nice, thank you. But only a small one,
as I'm driving,' she said lightly.

'Leave those things for now.' Nick waved a dismissive
hand towards the suitcase she had just closed. 'You can
collect them later,' he added.

The house was just the same, the sitting-room as warm
and cosy as she had made it six months ago, when they
had redecorated, and yet Gemini already felt like a visitor.
In fact, now that she knew she was going to see Nick again
tomorrow evening, she just wanted to leave.

As they sat drinking their drinks, even their conversation
was stilted. Nick asked her about work; Gemini did the
same where he was concerned. But neither of them was
particularly interested in the answer. Work, she was sure,
was the last thing on either of their minds!

This was awful, Gemini finally decided, swallowing
down her drink as quickly as possible before standing up
to leave. 'I don't want to be late,' she excused as Nick
looked up at her enquiringly.

'Of course not,' he acknowledged abruptly, standing up
himself to walk with her to the door. 'Give my regards to
Hugh and Alan.'

How did one say goodnight to the man who was your husband—and yet so obviously wasn't? Gemini wondered miserably. 'See you tomorrow,' she told him lightly.

He gave an inclination of his head. 'I'll look forward to it.'

Would he really? Gemini mused self-derisively as she drove to Hugh and Alan's apartment. Somehow she doubted it.

But *she* would. Because tomorrow night was the last chance she had to try and salvage her marriage. It might not work out, but it wouldn't be for want of trying on her part!

CHAPTER TWELVE

'MY GOD, Gemini, you look beautiful!' Nick came to an abrupt halt in the salon doorway as he took in her appearance.

She had certainly done her best to be so; her gown was long silver-coloured silk, with tiny flowers in silver embroidered into the material. Low-necked, with thin shoulder-straps, it suited her light tan to perfection. The colour gave an ebony sheen to her hair, her eyes appearing almost navy in contrast. Nick was right. It was a stunning gown, and she felt good in it.

And his remark about the way she looked took attention away from her racing pulse and shortness of breath at how handsome *he* looked, in his black evening suit and snowy white shirt. But she had told him not so long ago how handsome he looked in a dinner suit, only to be rebuked for the remark, so this evening she determined to keep her opinion to herself!

'Thank you.' She smiled at his compliment, determined there would not be any awkwardness between them tonight, as there had been at the house last night as they'd drunk sherry together. 'Although I'm not quite ready. I thought you said eight o'clock...?' She frowned after a glance at her watch showed it was only twenty minutes to eight.

Nick's mouth set grimly. 'I did. Something came up,' he added scathingly.

'Come inside,' Gemini invited in a slightly puzzled voice. 'Can I get you a drink?' she offered once they were in the confines of the salon's compact apartment.

He nodded. 'Perhaps you had better get us both one!' he muttered enigmatically.

Something had certainly rattled him, Gemini realised with a frown as she moved about the tiny kitchen pouring them both a glass of wine from the bottle of cool Chablis she had in the small refrigerator. She had intended offering Nick a glass of wine when he arrived anyway. She'd thought it would be a nice way to begin their evening together. But Nick looked more in need of the alcohol than the sharing of a pleasant pre-dinner drink that Gemini had anticipated!

'Did you have a good evening with Hugh and Alan last night?' Nick prompted interestedly once he had taken a much-needed sip of his wine.

The two of them were now sitting opposite each other in the two armchairs in the small sitting-room.

Gemini smiled ruefully; it was impossible to have anything else but a good time in the company of the two men. Especially when the two of them had decided it was going to be an evening to cheer her up. Both of them had set out to be entertaining—and had succeeded. And yet Gemini had been aware all the evening that there was something missing—and that 'something' was Nick, at her side...

'Very good, thank you.' She nodded, smiling at the memory, but all the time aware that Nick was evading talking about the reason he had arrived so early.

Nick looked at her intently. 'You know, maybe the two of us should have done this before,' he murmured thoughtfully.

She frowned. 'Done what?'

'Gone out to dinner alone together. Or taken walks, like we did on Sunday. Holidays too. All the things that normal couples do together,' he added grimly.

Gemini grimaced. 'We were never a "normal" couple.'

'Why weren't we?' Nick frowned.

She swallowed hard. 'I—' She broke off awkwardly. They hadn't even gone out to dinner yet—and if this conversation became too intense now, then they probably wouldn't get out at all! And not because of any pleasurable reasons...

'Why?' Nick prompted again hardily.

Gemini gave a wistful sigh, knowing that in this mood Nick was unstoppable. 'I think when we first married we were too aware of the reason we had married at all, and as time went on it was too late to change the ground rules that had been laid down in the beginning.'

'But eventually we did change them, Gemini,' Nick rasped. 'And a lot of good it did either of us—because the next day you left me!'

'Not because of that,' she protested instantly, determined there should be no misunderstanding about her feelings concerning the night they had spent together. 'I left—I left because of something else entirely.'

'Danny,' Nick bit out harshly.

'No,' she denied categorically.

'He telephoned me today, Gemini,' Nick said softly, watching her intently.

She nodded, not too surprised after her own visit from Jemima—although, typically, Danny had taken the easier option and used the telephone rather than a face to face confrontation with his brother!

'Could he possibly be the "something" that came up?' she guessed shrewdly, sadly seeing the evening out with Nick that she had been anticipating all day disappear out of the window.

'Like the proverbial bad penny,' Nick confirmed disgustedly.

Gemini chewed on her bottom lip. 'Could I hazard a guess that he told you about his marriage to Jemima next month?' Why else would Nick be looking so grim?

Nick drew in a deep breath, standing up to look at her with narrowed eyes. 'You know about that too?'

'From Jemima,' she confirmed ruefully. 'I now know about a lot of things I wasn't at all clear on when I made my decision to leave you on Tuesday!' she murmured self-derisively.

'What sort of things?' he prompted warily.

She drew in a ragged breath. 'The most important one is who Jessica's father is,' she told him bluntly.

This conversation, as she had guessed it would, was destroying any chance the two of them might have had of spending a pleasant evening together. But it was too late to do anything to stop this now. It just had to roll on to its conclusion—whatever that might be…

'Danny, of course,' Nick dismissed scathingly. 'He and Jemima have been living together for months.'

'Eight, according to Jemima.' Gemini nodded. 'But I didn't know that then—'

'I'm aware of that.' Nick sighed. 'Why do you suppose I found it so damned difficult to explain, when I knew Danny shared his apartment with someone, and that the someone was Jemima—and their baby daughter?' He shook his head. 'But at least you know now, I suppose,' he muttered grimly.

She nodded. 'Jemima told me. When she came to ask if the two of us would be witnesses at their wedding next month,' she added softly, looking intently at Nick. After all, the fact that Jemima was marrying Danny didn't mean Nick wasn't still in love with her. In fact, the way he was pacing the room like a caged lion seemed to imply that he was!

Nick's mouth firmed into a thin line, his eyes glittering deeply green. 'I trust you gave her the same answer that I gave Danny earlier this evening!'

'Which was?' she prompted gently.

'When pigs fly! When hell freezes over! When—'

'Okay, I get the message!' Gemini cut in ruefully.

'So did Danny,' Nick nodded tersely.

And none of what they had said so far gave her any idea how Nick felt about Jemima marrying his brother...!

Her heart ached as she gave him surreptitious looks from beneath lowered lashes. She wanted to smooth the frown from between his eyes, take the grimness away from that mouth that could give such pleasure—

Not now, Gemini, she inwardly rebuked herself as she felt herself becoming aroused just looking at Nick. She needed to keep her head—and her emotions—clear, if she were going to make any sense to him at all.

Nick looked down at her with narrowed eyes, his expression unfathomable now.

Gemini swallowed hard. 'What is it?' she prompted self-consciously. She knew her make-up wasn't complete yet; she hadn't had time to put on her lipgloss before he arrived. But, then again, he *was* early...

He looked away briefly, before turning back again determinedly. 'I really don't care any more whether you want to hear this from me or not—you are uniquely the most beautiful woman I have ever seen in my life!' he told her bluntly.

Gemini felt as if she'd had all the breath knocked out of her body. She moistened her suddenly dry lips before answering. 'And why shouldn't I want to hear it?' she prompted huskily. 'Every woman likes to be told she's beautiful.'

'But not necessarily by me,' he clarified hardily.

She didn't want to hear it from anyone else! In fact, it would be completely meaningless from anyone else...

She gave a rueful grimace. 'There was only one thing wrong with your compliment, Nick—I'm far from unique; Jemima and I are identical twins,' she reminded him bleakly. Wasn't it that fact that had prompted him into proposing to her in the first place?

He shook his head disgustedly. 'I have told you before—the two of you are absolutely nothing alike!'

Gemini looked away. 'I know I haven't behaved very well in the last few days, Nick, but please don't be hurtful,' she choked, burying her face in her hands. It was over. It was all over. 'I've always known that to you I could only ever be a pale substitute for Jemima—'

'A what?' Nick cut in incredulously, moving her hand away from her face to pull her to her feet in front of him. 'What the hell are you talking about, Gemini?' He looked down at her searchingly.

And Gemini looked back at him, but she couldn't see him clearly, tears blinding her vision. 'I'm talking about the fact that it's Jemima you've always loved!' She wrenched away from him. She couldn't bear to be that close to him and know that it was still her sister that he loved. 'You married me because Jemima and Danny made fools of us both—and also because, to look at, at least, I'm Jemima's double. What a disappointment it must have been to you to learn that we really are nothing alike!' she added self-derisively. 'Jemima is the one that glows with beauty, that oozes fun, the daring one, the one who takes the risks—and always wins!' she choked.

As her sister had won again now. It didn't matter that Jemima was marrying Danny, that the two of them had a child together—not when Nick still loved her!

It had gone very quiet in the room after her outburst, so quiet she could hear the ticking of the clock on the mantelpiece. Why didn't Nick say something? Anything! And then just go…

She had been a fool. She'd really believed that with Jemima and Danny safely married to each other at last perhaps there could be a chance for Nick and herself. Fool. Idiot. Dreamer!

'I married *you*, Gemini,' Nick began softly, 'because I went to dinner one evening sixteen months ago to meet my fiancée's sister—and realised that I had only fallen in love with the *look* of Jemima. It was her twin I really wanted!'

Gemini raised her head slowly, looking across at Nick with disbelieving tear-wet eyes, shaking her head slowly, in denial of what he was saying.

'It's the truth, Gemini,' Nick assured her huskily. 'I met Jemima when she came to interview me for some story she was doing, and just the look of her—!' He shook his head disbelievingly at the memory. 'Something inside me went *pow*! I was lost. Hook, line and sinker. I was thirty-eight years old, but in just one look I knew this was the woman I wanted to marry, that I wanted to spend the rest of my life with, that—'

'Stop it!' Gemini put both her hands over her ears. 'Don't be cruel, Nick! I don't deserve this.' She began to cry again.

The first she knew of Nick being close to her was when he removed her hands from over her ears, his hands gently cradling each side of her face as he smoothed the tears from her cheeks with his thumbs.

She opened her eyes to find him looking down at her intently, searchingly, but with something else in those emerald depths, something she was afraid to recognise...

'Oh, Gemini,' he groaned raggedly. 'I don't mean to hurt you. I've never wanted to hurt you.' He shook his head. 'I meant what I said a few minutes ago,' he said huskily. 'I had been engaged to Jemima only a matter of weeks, but the night I met you I knew it had to end, that I couldn't marry Jemima—because it was *you* I loved!'

Gemini inhaled sharply, and couldn't seem to breathe out again! Nick couldn't be saying this to her—could he...?

He gave a self-derisive, humourless laugh at her disbelieving expression. 'Incredible, isn't it?' His thumbs continued to caress her creamy cheeks as he looked intently down into her face. 'You're wrong about Jemima. She may be beautiful—how could she be anything else when the two of you are twins—but it didn't take me too long to discover that the fun and daring you talk of are actually only a cover for her selfishness. She takes her fun at other people's expense.' His mouth twisted. 'And to take those risks, and win, she had to step over other people—and she really doesn't care who it is she steps on! The way she just left Jessica at the weekend for you to look after is evidence of her complete selfishness. Danny's too,' he added scathingly. 'She and Danny are so much alike I think they actually deserve each other!' he muttered disgustedly.

She knew all those things about her sister—but she loved her anyway. And she had thought Nick did too...!

'Whereas you, my darling Gemini,' Nick continued gruffly, 'you really are beautiful, inside as well as out. You've never intentionally harmed anyone, and you never could, either,' he added with certainty.

Gemini shook her head. 'You couldn't have known that about me then,' she said dazedly.

If Nick were to be believed, he had fallen in love with her that evening they'd all had dinner together, sixteen months ago! *If* he were to be believed...?

'Oh, I knew that about you from that first evening, Gemini,' Nick murmured assuredly. 'I couldn't take my eyes off you,' he remembered ruefully. 'You were so warm, so—so— Can you imagine what it felt like, Gemini, to realise I was engaged to marry the wrong sister?' he continued. 'I had no idea how to even go about breaking the engagement, let alone how I was then going to approach you!' He shook his head. 'I was obsessed with it for weeks, trying to come up with some way I could break my en-

gagement to Jemima but still have you,' he recalled harshly.
'But in the end I didn't have to find a way out, because
Jemima and Danny, with their usual lack of concern for
anyone but themselves, did it all for me!'

'But—but—' Gemini swallowed hard. 'All this time…?'
She shook her head.

'Yes—all this time!' Nick echoed heavily. 'Do you have
any idea how much I've loved you, ached for you this last
year? Of course you don't,' he answered himself derisively.
'How could you possibly know? I may have married you
because I love you, but you only married me because of
Danny's relationship with Jemima!' He shook his head.
'This last year—I've wished for so long, Gemini, that you
would come to care for *me*!'

'But I did! I mean, I do,' Gemini corrected agitatedly as
Nick's eyes narrowed disbelievingly. 'Nick, I love you,'
she told him forcefully. 'I've loved you for months. I've
wished—hoped—longed for you to love me in return.' She
looked up at him with glowing blue eyes. 'I had no idea
that you already did!'

She still couldn't believe it. Was it really possible that
Nick had loved her all the time?

'What I felt for Danny was infatuation,' she went on
quickly, as Nick just continued to stare at her. 'He was so
unlike anyone else I had ever known. Or at least…I thought
he was. Actually, he's just a male version of Jemima.' She
frowned at the realisation.

She had always envied her twin, knew that with her spar-
kling personality and her obvious beauty Jemima was the
one everyone always gravitated towards; Gemini had always wished she were more like her twin. Was it possible
she had been attracted to Danny only because he had that
same magnetism, selfish though it was…?

'I never loved him, Nick,' she said with certainty. 'Yes,
I was hurt and humiliated when he and Jemima deceived

us the way that they did. But it took me only a matter of weeks of being married to you to realise what a better man you are, in every way,' she told him earnestly. 'Nick, I do love you. I love you so much that the last few days without you have like a living hell!' she confessed shakily.

'Then why leave me at all?' he demanded harshly.

She swallowed hard. 'I— You aren't going to like this,' she admitted with a pained grimace. Nick had said he loved her—miraculously! Unbelievably!—but would he still do so once she had confessed to believing Jessica was his child…?

He shrugged broad shoulders. 'I can't dislike it any more than I have being without you the last four days!'

Gemini chewed on her bottom lip. 'I—I thought Jessica was your child!' she burst out apprehensively.

Nick looked at her. And looked at her. And continued to look at her!

'I believed you still loved Jemima,' Gemini defended heatedly at his continued silence. 'And Jessica's eyes are changing from blue to green! And—'

'And *I* have green eyes…' Nick realised softly.

'Exactly,' she pounced gratefully. 'And—and—' She broke of dazedly as Nick began to laugh. Not a cynical or strained laugh, but a deep, throaty chuckle that reverberated around inside his chest. 'Nick…?' she finally questioned uncertainly, when his mirth seemed to go on for ever.

He shook his head, gathering her into his arms, her face buried against his chest. 'Green eyes run in my family, Gemini—my grandfather had them, my uncle too,' he murmured ruefully.

'I thought you were going to be so angry with me for thinking that about Jessica,' she admitted chokingly.

'Why the hell should I be angry with you when I've been suffering from the same mistaken idea about you and Danny since he telephoned the house last weekend?' he acknowledged self-disgustedly. 'I even rushed over here this evening because I was sure you still loved Danny and would be devastated at the idea of his marrying Jemima!' He shook his head. 'And all this time you've believed I was still in love with Jemima, too!'

Put like that, it did sound rather stupid. Especially when it seemed they were really in love with each other...

Nick grimaced. 'Emotional insecurity has a lot to answer for.'

Gemini raised her head and looked up at him. 'Do you really love me, Nick?' she prompted huskily, still half afraid to believe him.

His arms tightened about her possessively. 'So much that I ache with it,' he admitted gently. 'Gemini, I love you very much; will you please marry me?'

She gave a shaky laugh. 'We already are married,' she minded him softly, her eyes glowing with love.

He shook his head. 'I want us to be really married. I came back early from my business trip last weekend because I couldn't stand the way we were living any more. I decided I had to talk to you, ask you to be my wife in every sense—all the time hoping that if we had a real marriage, possibly children, in the end you would come to love me.'

That was what he had wanted to talk to her about! 'I thought you were going to ask me for a divorce,' she confessed emotionally. 'That you knew you had made a mistake by marrying me, that it was still Jemima you really wanted. And Jessica's existence only seemed to confirm that belief.'

Nick nodded. 'Because you thought she was my daughter. I want *our* child, Gemini, yours and mine,' he told her fervently. 'Hell, I'm going too fast again,' he muttered self-reprovingly. 'First of all I would like us to go on that honeymoon we never had. Paris, if you'd like it?' He looked down at her.

She had been to Paris several times on business, but she knew that would be nothing like going on honeymoon there with Nick. 'I would love that,' she agreed huskily.

'So would I,' Nick acknowledged, his arms tightening about her. 'I love you, Gemini Drummond, and *only* you. More than I believed it possible to love anyone.' Once again his hands cupped either side of her face as he looked down at her intently.

Gemini's face shone with a reflection of that complete love. 'I love you, Nick Drummond, and *only* you. More than I ever believed it possible to love anyone.' She echoed his words sincerely.

He drew in a ragged breath. 'Do you really want to go out to dinner?'

'Why?' But she knew the reason why, could see the desire she felt for Nick reflected in his eyes as he looked down at her with hungry need.

'Because although you look very sexy in pyjamas—you look even sexier *without* them!' he told her warmly.

She laughed huskily. 'In that case—who needs food?!' She returned Nick's kiss with a passion that matched his own.

They loved each other, and nothing would ever be allowed to come between them again, she vowed inwardly. Nothing!

EPILOGUE

'I DIDN'T think I could ever love you more than I did a year ago, when you told me you loved me, too,' Nick murmured throatily as his head rested against her naked breasts. 'But I do,' he acknowledged dazedly, absently stroking the warmth of her thigh in the aftermath of their lovemaking.

Gemini laughed huskily. 'There's so much more of me to love!'

Nick's hand moved possessively to her rounded body, a small protesting movement against his hand telling him that the tiny inhabitant did not like being disturbed in this way. 'Do you think it's a boy or a girl?' he murmured wonderingly as he watched those tiny movements beneath her silken flesh.

In her sixth month of pregnancy, Gemini knew that the last year of being Nick's wife, and having him as her husband, in the fullest sense of the words, had been the happiest she had ever known. And, as with Nick, her love for him had only intensified.

She looked down at him, one of her hands gently caressing the darkness of his hair. 'Or boys or girls, plural?' she suggested huskily.

'I don't—' Nick broke off, looking up at her sharply. 'Gemini...?' he said uncertainly as she gave him an answering glowing smile.

'The doctor seemed a little surprised at my—largeness at my check-up today, and decided to give me another scan—it appears there are *two* babies, not one!' she told Nick happily, ecstatic at the thought of having his children.

'Two?' he echoed huskily, swallowing hard. 'But I—you—'

She laughed at his completely dumbfounded expression. 'Don't look so surprised, Nick; I am a twin myself, after all.'

'Yes, but— I always thought you and Jemima—that it—'

'Did I forget to mention that my mother was a twin, too?' She rolled over, so the two of them were facing each other as their heads lay on the same pillow.

'Must have slipped your mind.' Nick nodded, starting to smile himself now that the first shock was over. 'Do you mind, Gemini? Two babies.' He shook his head dazedly at the realisation.

'Do you?' she returned indulgently.

'Hell, no!' His arms tightened about her. 'I can't imagine anything more wonderful than two little girls who look just like their mother!'

'Or two little boys who look just like their father,' she pointed out happily.

'Jessica is going to have her work cut out dealing with two cousins,' Nick laughed softly.

Jessica was a regular visitor to their home, as were her parents. Jemima and Danny actually seemed to have matured themselves during this year of marriage. Although Jessica, at almost fourteen months old, had definitely taken over as the boss in the family, with her parents' lives revolving around her now rather than themselves. Which was probably just as well!

'She's going to love it,' Gemini said with certainty.

'So am I.' Nick nodded. 'But not as much as I love you, Gemini,' he nodded gruffly.

'Or I you,' Gemini echoed softly.

And their family was made complete two months later when, without too much warning and slightly premature, as twins were apt to be, their identical baby sons were born...

Tyler Brides

It happened one weekend...

Quinn and Molly Spencer are delighted to accept three bookings for their newly opened B&B, Breakfast Inn Bed, located in America's favorite hometown, Tyler, Wisconsin.

But Gina Santori is anything but thrilled to discover her best friend has tricked her into sharing a room with the man who broke her heart eight years ago....

And Delia Mayhew can hardly believe that she's gotten herself locked in the Breakfast Inn Bed basement with the sexiest man in America.

Then there's Rebecca Salter. She's turned up at the Inn in her wedding gown. Minus her groom.

Come home to Tyler for three delightful novellas by three of your favorite authors: Kristine Rolofson, Heather MacAllister and Jacqueline Diamond.

HARLEQUIN®
Makes any time special ™

PHTB

VIVA LA VIDA DE AMOR!

They speak the language of passion.

In Harlequin Presents®, you'll find a special
kind of lover—full of Latin charm. Whether
he's relaxing in denims or dressed for dinner,
giving you diamonds or simply sweet dreams,
he's got spirit, style and sex appeal!

Latin Lovers is the new miniseries
from Harlequin Presents® for anyone
who enjoys hot romance!

Meet gorgeous Antonio Scarlatti in
THE BLACKMAILED BRIDEGROOM
by Miranda Lee, Harlequin Presents® #2151
available January 2001

And don't miss sexy Niccolo Dominici in
THE ITALIAN GROOM
by Jane Porter, Harlequin Presents® #2168
available March 2001!

Available wherever Harlequin books are sold.

HARLEQUIN®
Makes any time special ™

Visit us at www.eHarlequin.com   HPLATIN

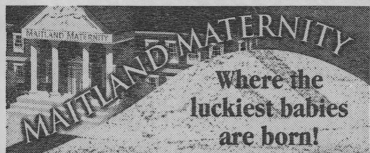

If you enjoyed what you just read,
then we've got an offer you can't resist!

Take 2 bestselling
love stories FREE!
Plus get a FREE surprise gift!

#1 *New York Times* bestselling author

NORA ROBERTS

brings you more of the loyal and loving,
tempestuous and tantalizing Stanislaski family.

Coming in February 2001

The Stanislaski Sisters

Natasha and Rachel

Though raised in the Old World traditions of their
family, fiery Natasha Stanislaski and cool, classy
Rachel Stanislaski are ready for a *new* world of love....

*And also available in February 2001 from
Silhouette Special Edition, the newest book in the
heartwarming Stanislaski saga*

CONSIDERING KATE

Natasha and Spencer Kimball's daughter Kate turns her
back on old dreams and returns to her hometown, where
she finds the *man* of her dreams.

Available at your favorite retail outlet.

Where love comes alive™

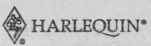

HARLEQUIN®

makes any time special—online...

eHARLEQUIN.com

your romantic escapes

Indulgences

- ♥ Monthly guides to indulging yourself, such as:
  - ★ Tub Time: A guide for bathing beauties
  - ★ Magic Massages: A treat for tired feet

Horoscopes

- ♥ Find your daily Passionscope, weekly Lovescopes and Erotiscopes

- ♥ Try our compatibility game

Reel Love

- ♥ Read all the latest romantic movie reviews

Royal Romance

- ♥ Get the latest scoop on your favorite royal romances

Romantic Travel

- ♥ For the most romantic destinations, hotels and travel activities

Harlequin proudly brings you

STELLA CAMERON
Bobby Hutchinson
Sandra Marton

in

MARRIED IN SPRING

*a brand-new anthology in which three couples
find that when spring arrives, romance soon
follows...along with an unexpected
walk down the aisle!*

February 2001

Available wherever Harlequin books are sold.

HARLEQUIN®
Makes any time special™

Visit us at www.eHarlequin.com   PHMARRIED